EVEN *Angels* NEED MIRACLES

A.C. MOORE

MooreNovels.com

This book dedicated to my family.

(Immediate, Extended, and Spiritual)

A special note to the reader ...

Thank you for placing this book in your hands. I'm humbled that you're giving me the opportunity to share this story with you. I must ask one favor from you - please tell others about Even Angels Need Miracles or MooreNovels.com. Anything you can do to help, whether it's word of mouth, sharing the Web site or or forwarding the book trailer, I appreciate it all. Thank you again.

A FEW THOUGHTS AND THANK YOUS

I've never believed in luck or coincidence. I believe there is a time, a place and a purpose for everything. For every failure and success, for good times and bad times; for strengths and weaknesses, there is a reason and meaning. While I do not always know the meaning in that moment, I've come to trust that the God who loves me, allows certain experiences, at certain times for my ultimate good fortune. I also believe the same for you.

I am thrilled to have completed my second novel. I'm even more thrilled that it is now in your hands.

Following my first novel, *Always Room for Dessert*, I have received much encouragement to write another. To my family, friends, neighbors, and colleagues, thanks for the support. I want to mention a few individuals – not in any particular order – who helped me by serving in a specific role ...

Dorothy Boulware – for editing. Dorothy is the editor of Mustard Seed Magazine, a great spiritual read. Visit mustardseedmag.org for more information and I encourage you to subscribe.

Zizwe Allette – for my photo shoot. This guy is sick with the camera. Very creative and passionate about his work. He's a talented photographer and a good friend. He's also for hire. See some of his work at www.flickr.com/zizwe

Perry Sweeper – for the cover design and page layout. Perry is a true creative, professional and patient with his clients. I'm elated about the design. Interested in his work? Email him at psweeper@gmail.com

www.SitesinOneDay.com – for helping me get MooreNovels.com going. Sites In One Day .com (SitesinoneDay.com – no spaces of course) is the real deal. Not only is the company adept in Web building, but they have real people skills. They listen and ask questions to build what you want. Check them out.

My sister Lettemariam (Letta) Moore and my close friend Diane Hocker – for reading the first draft and giving me honest feedback. It's always good to have people in your corner that will give constructive criticism.

My children Kayla, Karah, and Kameryn Moore – for talking with me about the book and giving me plenty of ideas every morning while driving them to school and daycare.

My wife Oprah – for letting me interrupt her thoughts, workday and sometimes sleep to bother her with ideas for the book and detailed description for every step of the process.

And last but far from least, to God the Father – for giving me this story to tell and the talent and determination to get it done. Thank you, I especially could not have done this without any of you.

As I said before, I don't believe in things just happening. All of you have become a part of my life, perhaps for such a time as this. Thank you all for being there.

Peace,

PROLOGUE

Nothing sounds more like death than the zip of a body bag. Ask anyone who's watched a corpse being taken away and they'll tell you the zip of a body bag has a different sound than that of luggage preparing for vacation or a warm down-filled coat to fend against the cold. A body bag zip is deep. It's hollow. And no matter how fast it's zipped, it's always slow and dragging. When they zipped the bag to a close, Aalon recognized the finality of the situation. The paramedics wheeled the body out of the door and loaded it onto the van. The now ex-girlfriend understandably suffered shock from the sudden death of Sean Logan. Though only moments ago she screamed for someone to stop him, and to help her, she didn't want it to end like this. The ambulance carted her away to the hospital only minutes ago. She was still puzzled how, with no warning at all, Sean tripped in his rage and fell four stories over the banister to his death.

Aalon struggled to do all he could to keep Sean from dying and after his efforts failed, he did all he could to try to bring him back. There was not a lot of time to respond and there were far more people around than he would have liked. Certainly, this interrupted divine order. Why did this happen? On his knees he sat limp like a wilted flower. His head hung partly in guilt, partly in exhaustion. To say he did everything in his power was an understatement.

Unlike ever before, questions, thoughts, doubt; they all kept pestering his mind. The luminous aura that surrounded him with what looked like wings of light began to fade into a shadowy covering, casting what appeared to be a darkened cape behind him. Though Aalon had not completely lost hope, he certainly lost some assurance that all was in control.

Mistake, he thought to himself. Certainly not done intentionally, but can something of this magnitude be a mistake? Aalon predicted an impact beyond measure from this first-time happening. He knew he needed to tell the council of angels, though it wouldn't surprise him if they already knew. They tend to know everything – especially things he and others wished they didn't.

As he looked at his shaking hands, he replayed the event over again in his mind. His nervous breathing and wandering thoughts made it hard for him to see clearly. He couldn't determine where he went wrong or what he could have possibly done differently. He did everything he should have done. Or so it seemed.

"He tried to kill her," he quietly said to himself as if to calm his own inner convictor.

There wasn't anything else he could say to give him even a distant sense of relief. The truth of the matter is this is a terrible thing – a thing so terrible, it could most certainly wipe out the faith of all mankind.

In the past, Aalon did admit to being angry, even furious with his human assignment Sean. He, from time to time, did share his frustration with other angels and through his prayers, but he did not wish for him to die. Sean was traveling on a fast path to destruction for quite some time. His risky behavior and violent antics kept his life in danger. His girlfriend of three years, tried to influence him to do better, but nothing she did seemed to have any lasting impact. When she decided to leave him to his own vices, he became drunk with rage and decided to teach her a lesson – the permanent kind. With gun in hand, he aimed and was intent on squeezing the trigger. Aalon tried to discourage him. He tried to slow him. He wanted to stop him. Though Aalon thought he barely nudged

Sean during his sinful rampage, apparently that nudge had more force behind it then he thought. He didn't expect him to go sailing over the banister. He could still hear his scream as he fell twisting through the narrow eye of the apartment spiraling stair case. The fractured skull and broken neck that came from the impact of falling four floor levels gave death an easy win – only minor twitches and then permanent stillness. Aalon wanted to soar down and catch him, but with so many witnesses, there was no way to save him inconspicuously. Sean landed on the side of his head and then his back. The eyes and facial expression, though no longer containing life, showed total surprise – and sadness. As Aalon reflected in silence, a cold stillness fell over the room.

"Murder Aalon?" Iblis, the Prince of Darkness rose out of the shadow cast by the grandfather clock in the foyer and whispered with a rasp. He could see Aalon kneeling over. He couldn't tell if he was praying or crying. Whatever the case, he took pleasure in knowing he would soon interrupt his private moment. Iblis took a few small steps and quietly knelt beside Aalon. Not wanting to startle Aalon and ruin the beautiful masterpiece of a saddened angel before him, he hesitated to reach out to him and then as if he were a father consoling his son, he extended his arm and slender, almost bony fingers to softly comb through Aalon's hair. He said, as compassionately as possible, "There's nothing you can do now. He's gone. You're welcome to stay with me."

Aalon neither cried nor prayed. Instead he silently sat in a meditative state – almost dazed – still pondering the untimely death, when the evil Iblis' presence finally registered.

"Leave," Aalon said faintly. While on his knees at the site of the fall, his stare still focused on the spot where Sean landed. Iblis ignored the request. He wasn't quite sure if Aalon was talking to him or suggesting to himself what he should do next.

"LEAVE!" he yelled again, as he flung Iblis' hand off and stood up in a fury ready to charge. His tightly held fists shook for violence. He took one step, and then hesitated to take another. His fists released their tense state. He realized he might be making another mistake – this time in anger. Iblis threw his hands up in a cowering fashion as if to show fear. He so wanted Aalon to take the bait. Only a few seconds transpired between their stares, then in a soundless flicker Aalon sprung into the air making his way to the rooftop, where he screamed to the heavens in anger, "Why!" He fell to this knees again and sobbed. Not wanting to pass up the opportunity to rub salt in Aalon's wounds, Iblis leaped high into the ceiling and joined Aalon on the roof. Aalon turned around and before Iblis could say anything, he took off once more. Iblis gave chase and soon the current and fallen angels hovered over the house, then higher over the neighborhood, beyond the trees, the city skyline and into the clouds. A flury of wind and bursts of light surrounded the two as they climbed higher and faster than humanly possible. Though they were in a spiritual state, the intense speed caused both hair and clothing to flutter in the wind.

"You're not welcome there," Iblis said grabbing Aalon's ankle. He tried to slow him down but couldn't. "You're a fool to go to heaven. They've no tolerance for imperfection and you and I certainly know you are far from that – especially now."

"I will face my judgment," Aalon turned and said proudly. "That's the difference between me and you!" He gritted his teeth as he kicked his ankle free to climb faster and higher, beyond the blackness and silence of space. As Aalon's breathing grew more into gasping, he continued to sprint his way to heaven to deliver the news in person. He traveled faster still to get away from Iblis. He hated hearing his laughter and taunts. Iblis stopped his own ascension just above the E arth's atmosphere. His laughter and screaming echoed in Aalon's mind.

"There's no difference between us! You've done the unthinkable! Not only have you hand delivered a soul to me, you've done what even I couldn't imagine. This news brings the leverage I've always sought. It changes everything – everything!" His laughter grew more intense, interrupting all of Aalon's thoughts. "A guardian angel murders the one he's assigned to protect! Thank you, Aalon. You've just handed me the battle and given me victory!"

Those words penetrated Aalon's ears, and more tears began to well. He paused outside the gates of heaven hoping for entry. Please open, he thought to himself. Albeit, it took a moment, the gate slowly swung open. With tears, a sigh and some reluctance, he walked through.

CHAPTER 1

Athyna left the angelic council abruptly. Her respect for their authority evaporated almost as quickly as she left. She could not stand the tone or direction of the conversation. Could it be that they actually seemed frightened by Iblis and prepared to side with is reasoning? She could not stand there and listen to his spewed lies and twisted truth as if he really intended to have honest dialogue. She hoped they were still picking up the scattered scrolls and other remnants that fell to the floor after she flipped the table over in a wrath and stormed out of the hall. Despite their warnings of her getting involved, she was determined to make good on her promise and get Aalon the help he needed, since they obviously were too afraid. They sickened her. Her several outbursts not only embarrassed the council in front of The Dark One, but also and mostly Jericho, an advisor and the one angel that convinced the council to allow her to attend the discussion. Though he suspected this gathering would be tough for her, she pleaded for permission to attend and knowing her closeness to Aalon, he sided against his own better judgment. He was the only one to follow her back to her sanctuary.

"Have you lost your mind Athyna?" Jericho roared as he slammed the door behind him with an almost paralyzing force. "Look at me! I can't support this abomination - this illicit personal pursuit! Never mind the council, do not overstep HIS grace! You will unleash more harm than help."

Athyna's mind overflowed with certainty. While the determined side of her thought process wanted her to get away from Jericho, the common sense portion was glad he followed. Though in total opposition to her, he truly did represent the last chance for practical thinking. She knew that the outcome of this behind-the-door, away from the angelic council discussion, would either aid her with comfort in the continuation of her plan, or convince her that this idea qualified as demented.

With all the internal confusion, anxiety, frustration and fear beginning to build, something inside her called for Jericho to convince her to abandon this unauthorized and certainly uncharted mission. She desperately wanted an easier option.

Athyna barely looked toward Jericho's direction. She started to speak – her voice, accompanied by her small feminine frame came out as a weak, tearful whisper.

"When I asked you of this possibility, you said it has never happened. You called it uncertain." She walked over to her window to bask in the brilliant, constant light, but unlike all other times in the past, she found no peace in the warm radiance. Sensing her discomfort, Jericho stepped closely behind her and gently placed his hand on her shoulder. He could feel her shoulders release a good portion of tension and that she took comfort in knowing he was nearby.

"Yes, I said those things, but –"

"Well, I think we need a little uncertainty now," she interrupted. "Because the one certain thing we do know is Aalon will fall at the hands of The Dark One if we do nothing! So maybe, we should seek the unthinkable. Perhaps this time we should exercise some faith."

Though he could see the desperation in her eyes, Jericho wrestled with the notion of supporting her decision. He struggled to say something, but could not find comforting words. For the second time in his existence, he felt what humans described as fear and he hated it. Something strange and distressing existed in "not knowing." He often considered those in the flesh world who managed to act on hope and faith as remarkable. Athyna's comments were awkward and surprising. As an angel, what did she know about faith? Knowledge eclipsed any need for faith in an angel's world – and from knowledge came obedience. While angels didn't know everything, the fact that their orders from on high were loud and clear, resulting in knowledge rather than just a strong internal belief that humans relied on, always made up for any feelings of uncertainty.

Every angel in heaven dreaded the recent news of Aalon, a guardian angel accused of allowing, some say causing an 'untimely death' to happen during his watch. The Dark One chose to use the word "murder" in his description. Earlier, Jericho addressed the members of the angelic council, and encouraged them to give Aalon the benefit and fairness of a hearing. A myriad of questions floated about the death, and the fate of Aalon, not to mention all of humanity. The possible chain of events that could result already started forming in the imagination of many. Not one angel wanted to see Aalon as a fallen or an outcast, yet none took it upon themselves to do anything, which bothered Athyna to her core. She stood determined do something. Jericho appreciated her zeal, but thought she flirted with making a colossal error in judgment. One doesn't correct a mistake with another mistake, he thought.

"Athyna, I think you should reconsider. Let time bring about a solution." He knew she wouldn't buy into his words. Even he didn't find much comfort in them.

"I do not trust time right now," Athyna responded. She reflected on the argument Iblis raised at the council hearings. Not only did he accuse Aalon of killing his guarded human out of frustration, he also accused the angel council of favorable bias toward Aalon and any angel who would represent him in the high courts. As a guardian angel, Aalon would not stand a chance representing himself against the calculating, cunning adversary. Aalon's situation looked bleak indeed. Athyna looked Jericho in the eye. "This could be our answer."

Jericho could tell Athyna didn't want to compromise. She wanted his full support. He needed to choose.

"If you plan to approach who I think, we will need to talk to one who is here now," Jericho finally stared into Athyna's eyes. He even smiled. "Follw me."

"Thank you," Athyna sobbed. "This means everything to me." She hugged Jericho. He hugged her back. Jericho's hug gave Athyna the warmth and strength she needed - just short of the confidence that a hug from the Great One himself provided.

"It will not come easy. You will not be permitted to show the miracles you normally are afforded – not for your own message.

Athyna just stared in surprise. "You mean I have to go in the flesh?"

"I'm not sure what I mean," he responded. "I just know you will need to be careful. Perhaps you will be protected, perhaps not. If you do meet harm, The Dark One will seek to extinguish you."

Athyna closed her eyes, "I know. I willl be careful."

They walked out of the room together preparing to mark another first in history – Athyna, a messenger angel, who for centuries received missions to deliver a word from above, was to deliver her own message to a selected human on Earth.

CHAPTER 2

"Has the jury reached its verdict," Judge Andy Toliver asked. A trying four days of testimony and deliberation finally came to an end, bringing anxiety and I'm sure much needed relief to many in the courtroom. Solomon Shivers held my hand tightly. His wife and grandson, sat in complete desperation. You could almost hear their heart beating in the same staccato pattern. I couldn't tell if the beads of sweat forming on Solomon's wrinkled face were from nervousness or from the overheated courtroom. Though February brought on a heavy chill in Baltimore, the courtroom seemed unusually warm. The forty-year-old courthouse had a climate control system that only had two settings, hot or cold.

"Yes we have your honor," the jury foreman said standing straight as an attentive soldier. He pulled the small index card from his pocket and adjusted his bifocals before beginning to read. "We the jury, find the defendant, Solomon Shivers, not guilty."

A wave of relief rushed through my chest like always. I knew we presented a fair and sensible case, but you never can be sure how a jury will vote when deliberating. Their 35 minutes were the longest I've had to wait out in a long time. A couple of disbelieving attendees made loud gestures, but none of them was louder than the judge's gavel that ended the trial.

"Tha-tha thank, y-y-you sssso much," Solomon said. Though his stuttering stood permanent through the entire trial, it became calmer at the sound of the verdict read in his favor. I reflected on his testimony, as he gave the jurors a first-hand convincing glimpse at the kind of torment he had faced for years.

"And what did you tell them when they said they wouldn't get off your car," I asked.

"I-I-I t-t-told them I w-w-would c-call the po-po-lice," he said.

Solomon Shivers lived as a retired installer for the local cable company. He, his wife and grandchildren lived modestly in a small blue-collar part of Baltimore City. By many, he was seen as a quiet, respectful resident. He often kept to himself. He took pride in his home making sure his yard was neatly groomed and his front porch was tidy. All his life, he worked hard to meet his family's needs. As the neighborhood began to take a turn for the worse, the local teens, some say gangs, would annoy Solomon daily by sitting on the hood of his car and dropping a piece of litter on his front, just to hear him stutter his request for them to stop. When his teenage grandson, Byron, came to his defense one day, he too became a target receiving threats at school and name calling. One day as Byron was washing the car, the group of teenagers jumped him, Solomon came out with his gun and fired some shots in the air, startling the teens. Greg Jackson, one of the teens often harassing Solomon, and a local high school basketball star, ran in the street and met an oncoming truck causing permanent hip damage forcing him into a wheelchair. Greg's popularity in the neighborhood and among high school sports enthusiasts gave him support as he sued for damages, his family and lawyers claimed he lost his chance of landing a basketball scholarship for college. There were rumors that a university had sunk a lot of money into his coffers, as a means to persuade him to attend their school. Greg obviously spent the money and the university was trying to get at least a portion back through the lawsuit. While there was no official paper trail of spending, the university definitely showed a willingness to lend its resources to assist Greg. Several interviews in the local media with the university's coaching staff and athletic director all but painted Greg as a saint with a promising sports career. During Solomon's testimony, supporters of Greg mocked, laughed and teased him loudly. Even Greg's mother, who should have set a better example, joined in the ruckus. A frustrated Judge Toliver had to interrupt Solomon's testimony to get order in the room several times. Eventually, a few of Greg's friends needed to be escorted from the courtroom. They behaved exactly as I hoped. During the closing argument I didn't even have to look at my notes.

"Ladies and Gentlemen of the jury, earlier today you saw a glimpse of what my client goes through on a daily basis. The laughter; the mocking; the insults; the disrespect; Mr. Shivers is always a target. For years, this man who never bothered anyone, who never had a run-in with the law, who worked faithfully until his retirement, would come home, like many of us, and hear the swearing, abuse and nastiness daily. I'm sure he wishes he could have them escorted away much like you witnessed Judge Toliver do today," I paused and turned to the judge for dramatic effect. "But Solomon is a patient man. He's gentle. Over and over again, he would talk to them. He'd talk to their parents and other family. Sometimes, he'd call the police – yet, nothing changed. This is the same man that used that very car those teens would sit on, to take them out for ice cream or to baseball game with his grandson when they were younger."

I could tell that brought shame to some of the young men who were left in the room and made Greg especially a little uneasy. Perhaps they had a conscious after all. "When they scratched his car and slashed his tires, he reported it to the police and had it fixed with his own money. Not until they physically assaulted his grandson, a four on one fight mind you, did Solomon come outside on his porch and fire a gun in the air. Remember, one foot was still in his house. With all of his frustration, he could have come outside fully, or taken aim, but he didn't. He merely scared them away. Greg Jackson the oldest of the bunch was scared so badly, he ran through the street and missed seeing the oncoming truck."

I continued describing how Solomon and his grandson ran to Greg's aid, called 911 and stayed with him until the paramedics came. I talked about Solomon's and his grandson's visit to the hospital only to have them refused entry and blamed for Greg's injury. In under 20 minutes, I wrapped up what I thought was a brilliant closing. Immediately after I walked back to take my seat, I overheard one person say it served him right. I put my arm around Solomon to let him know he did a good job earlier. I could tell his stuttering still brewed embarrassment for him. And though I kind of felt bad for putting Solomon on the stand, it did do what I needed.

Rosie, Solomon's wife, jarred me out of my thoughts about the case with a tight hug. "Thank you Erin! Thank you so much!" She said. She extended her long arms to scoop up her husband and grandson in the embrace. "How can we make this up to you?"

Immediately, I could have asked her to let go of the group hug. I was beginning to lose my balance. A small part of me wanted to revise our contract and ask for more money, but I knew from the start Solomon didn't have a lot of money to spend. His retirement income and social security did not go far, especially with him now taking care of his grandson and younger sister, whose parents weren't able to handle the responsibility.

"It's okay, really," I said. Rosie finally turned the hug loose. I gave Solomon a firm handshake and placed a hand on his shoulder. "Just promise me you'll keep the gun indoors."

Solomon looked at me with a smile. "I promise," he said without stuttering.

"Then, that's all I need to hear," I got suckered into another Rosie-orchestrated group hug. This time, I ended it. I was ready to leave and I knew deep down, they wanted to get out of the courtroom and put this behind them.

"Go ahead and get out of here. We'll get together in a few days to sign final papers."

As the Shivers family, court witnesses and officials began leaving, I saw Kevin Banneker standing in the back row folding his overcoat over his arm. No surprise there. His 6'3, wide shouldered frame made him look like a giant among the rest of the spectators, and as usual he took the best dressed award. His tie, watch, shoes, and coat worked the suit to perfection – everything coordinated perfectly. He caught me looking and then silently clapped in favor of my victory. For a good while now, Kevin made a habit of just popping up - today in court, last week in church and a few days before that, he actually came to my yoga class. Only recently did he start attending my trials. If he and I didn't go way back, I definitely would have called the police and filed a harassment claim and restraining order.

"Another impressive win," he said walking toward me; his hand ready to grasp mine. As he walked past others leaving, we soon became the last two in the courtroom. Kevin continued to seek my interest in joining the Hoffman and Dudley law group. I smiled, shook his hand and my head at the same time. "That should put you at exactly 43 wins. We could use you and more importantly, you could use us." He stared at my dated laptop with the system error message on the screen. I folded it close and placed it and my legal pad in my bag as he walked me to the door. I could smell the cologne pleasantly. Even, the hall outside the courtroom was starting to become empty. I checked my watch it was exactly 5:15 p.m. I should definitely walk quickly and move my car, from the meter, I thought to myself. We turned in my badge to the security desk and made our way further to the exit. The bare halls made for a slightly eerie echo effect.

"Have you at least considered," Kevin asked while we slowly walked down the hall passing a few janitors beginning to get started.

"Considered what?" I responded. "If you're still asking whether I'm interested in joining the firm my answer is still the same."

"Erin, please," he said. "This is a good look. I've been with Dudley and Hoffman for four years and I'm in line to make partner soon. You could really take off at the firm. Besides I can't stand to see my girlfriend struggle."

"I'm not struggling and I haven't' been your girlfriend since the eighth grade." Though his smile forced a smile from me, I cut it short to drive my point confidently.

"Well, I never broke up with you," Kevin said jokingly, "and I know you didn't break up with this." He pointed to himself as if he were somehow God's gift to me.

I just stared as if he lost his mind, however it didn't take long for my smile to return "Kevin, you're wasting your time. There are other lawyers who I'm sure would love to be a part of your team."

"But they aren't the best," he said while walking closer to me. His voice dropped to a base-filled whisper. "And I only want the best." There he goes again with that perfect balance of professional and personal courtship, I thought.

"Don't you mean Dudley and Hoffman want the best," I asked.

"Them too." He took my hand drawing me just a tad closer to him, grazing my cheek with a soft playful kiss.

I politely pulled away heading for the door.

"Can we discuss this over dinner?" Kevin followed me.

"We did that already," I said. I reached for the door and as soon as I opened it to step out, a young woman entered.

"Excuse me, Erin Crawford?" The woman asked.

I must admit I was startled having her call my name as if she knew I was coming out. "Yes, do I know you?" I tried to place her face. There was something familiar, but nothing that jumped out. Everything about her seemed troubled; her whisper, quick movements and constant surveying the hall gave her an almost paranoid demeanor. She looked like she had run on hard times.

"I need your help."

Kevin caught up to the both of us. "Is everything okay," he asked.

"We're okay." I handed a business card to her which read Erin Crawford – Attorney at Law. One of my pet peeves is being asked for representation, while at the courthouse – especially after a long day of work.

"I'm sorry. I'm kind of in a rush." I said. "Here's my card. You can give my office a call to set up an appointment." I smiled to let her know that I wasn't trying to be rude or blow off hearing more from her, but at the same time, I was truly ready to leave.

I handed my card to her. She looked down at the card for a brief second and then gently grabbed my hand.

"Erin, I need to talk to you. It's extremely important." She had the kind of voice that sounded as though tears were closely behind. Something in this woman made me want to listen to at least a brief story.

"What's wrong?" I asked.

"A serious trouble is growing--"

"Ma'am, we're closing," the security officer said as he walked toward us, cutting the young woman off in mid-sentence. "You're going to have to exit the building."

We stepped outside just in time to see a silver Volkswagen Passat being towed away.

"No!" I shouted. My eyes followed the flatbed truck as it turned the corner out of sight. I turned to look at Kevin.

"I got you," he said. "But we have to leave now. I don't think I have many minutes left on my meter either."

"Look, I have to go, but call me and we can talk" I said to the woman. I started to walk off with Kevin before turning around to see the woman one more time. "What's your name?"

She stared at the card without answering.

CHAPTER 3

A cold February rain filled the night. Steam rose from just about every manhole cover and no one but the unlucky were in the streets.

Though it was three o'clock in the morning, the frantic knocking compelled Sister Mary to answered the door. She immediately recognized the mother child combination standing in front of her.

"Oh goodness, come in, come in," she answered in the sort of excitement that the tired hour of three a.m. would barely allow. The young woman walked in carrying her sleeping four-year-old over her shoulder – her crying, barely audible. Sister Mary pushed the door shut and locked it. She walked toward the young woman to show her to her room. She noticed the black eye and bruised cheekbone. Only a week ago, the young woman came in and said she needed help. She stayed a few days and decided to go back to her boyfriend and work out their differences.

After the woman laid the child on the twin bed next to hers, she leaned toward the shorter Sister Mary to give her a hug.

"Thank you," she whispered, her crying much more apparent now.

"It's quite all right, my child," she responded in kind. She gently patted her back and rocked in a comforting sway. "I'll bring you some ice for your swelling.

Change out of those wet clothes. I have a warm night gown in the drawer and something for your son too. You must be tired. We can talk next steps tomorrow."

"I'm so sorry Sister Mary."

"Shh, not to worry," Sister Mary interrupted with a whisper. "Let's not wake the baby. Tomorrow. We can talk tomorrow. You and your son need rest. I'll go get the ice."

After leaving the room, Sister Mary turned down the hall toward the kitchen for ice as she promised. It seems every week, it's the same story with different characters. She was certain her help to these young women made a difference, yet inside there was confusion and emptiness. The kind of emptiness she thought was too deep even for God to fill. After joining the convent 43 years ago at the early age of 22 years old, many of her sisters wondered if it was her never really having a young life of her own that held her back from fully enjoying her worship and service. If only that was the case. If her sisters knew what led her to join in the first place, they probably would toss her out. She stared at her reflection in the microwave almost in disgust. She was sure that even God considered her service vain. She put a few cubes in a zip lock bag and headed back to the room.

Anytime you wake up with pillow case crease marks on your face, you know you had a good night's rest. I sat up and thought of how kind Kevin was to take me to get my car. He even offered to help me pay the $250 to get it back. I should have taken him up on that offer I thought, since he was partly the reason I was late leaving court, but he would have only used that to make a case for me to join the firm. I looked at the clock, which read 8:30 a.m. With the Shivers'

trial now out of the way I could focus on organizing. Usually after bringing a case to a close, I take the next day to just catch up and enjoy the calm before the next storm. Check messages, reading a few magazines and journals and planning for the rest of the week was on my agenda. It was a jeans and hoodie day but still an important one.

I took one final stretch, got cleaned up and dressed before walking down the steps to my office to scroll through my messages and all the forms of mail that had my name on it. Creaking stairs and the sounds of traffic and construction began to fill my ears with each step. After finally making it to my desk I discovered more bills than I cared to see, including a third notice for property taxes and an overdue water bill. I shook my head at how much money I owed to the city. Among all my mounting debt, I received an invitation to join a legal association and a few requests for representation - most asking for free or discounted service.

"I guess the word is getting out," I said to myself sarcastically. "I'm officially known as the lawyer who pimps herself." Four years at Lincoln University, four years at Temple and with loans still to pay off, one would think getting paid top dollar for my services would look real appealing, but I'm cursed by the influence of my grandmother, who constantly reminded me of the importance of giving. I had just deleted my old messages when Audrey walked in the front door, carrying a cup of coffee and a laundry bag. Audrey was my young foster sister, who I grew up with in this very house.

"Whew, it's cold out there," she said. It was the first week of February and the coldest it's been since winter started.

"Well close the door so you don't let the heat out."

As she set the bag behind her desk, one of my apartment tenants, Yvonne rang the buzzer. I buzzed her inside and she walked in to hand me the rent. She always pays on time and never gives me any trouble.

"I haven't heard much music lately," I said referring to her keyboard rehearsal. Yvonne was the church choir director for Great Faith Baptist Church. To see and hear such a small woman – barely five foot, belt out such a mature and melodious voice was phenomenal. On some nights she could be heard singing gospel hymns, while playing piano. Often I found myself listening to her rehearse. The older songs, she would sing reminded me of my grandmother, as she would hum or sing a gospel tune from time to time.

"I've been studying," she said humbly. Yvonne was studying to become an ordained minister. "I have one more exam before finishing seminary."

"Good for you. I'm glad one of the students in this building is studying," I said while turning to Audrey.

"I study," she said defensively. "Just not in the traditional sense. I observe my knowledge through everyday life and not through a book. Now, changing the subject, please don't forget the lock smith will be by today to change the lock on your door," Audrey said.

"That's right," Yvone said. "I'll be back around lunch to get the new key. Since this evening I have a rehersal and may not be back before you close the office."

"That's fine. I'll be here, just buzz the front, I'll let you in," Audrey said.

"Have a good day," Yvonne said before heading out. "And don't worry, I'll be playing and singing again in no time. We have a special performance coming up soon at the church. So, I definitely better get my playing and singing in shape."

I watched as she left for work in the cold with the warmest smile on her face. In some ways, Yvonne reminded me a lot of myself. I'm guessing with her voice and talent, she could have made a high paid career and name for herself by crossing over in to R&B or at least serving as choir director for any number of the mega churches in the area, but instead, she served in a small old church a few miles away in one of Baltimore's most needy neighborhoods. Without that church, the neighborhood would be even more distressed. She continued walking and was soon out of my sight.

My grandmother gave me this old corner row home after I graduated from law school, right before she died. Over the years, I've had a lot of rennovations made. I'm told when she bought it more than 50 years ago, it was just under

$50,000. Today I've had offers for almost 10 times that amount. It's big enough to house two apartments, including my own and a small but comfortable law office. In New York, this would certainly fetch close to a million dollars. It's the perfect home for me, but without the steady checks from Yvonne, it would be way too much property for a small-time lawyer to maintain.

"I see you got your messages," Audrey said, while powering her laptop. Audrey used her own because the computer I had at her desk was more than a few years old. She tried to spare my feelings by claiming her laptop was needed for studying, but from what I saw it provided faster access to Facebook.

At 21 years old, Audrey was in her senior year at Morgan State University majoring in political science and looking forward to law school. Since her freshmen year, I've given her part-time work to "keep gas in her car" as she puts it.

"Are we going to take the Antonio Walker case," she asked knowing full well the answer.

I just looked at her.

"Aw come on Erin. The dude's got crazy loot."

"I try not to represent criminals."

"Objection, prejudice."

"Overruled. He's already pleaded guilty on drug distribution. The article also says he has an attempted murder charge. "

I tossed her the newspaper so she could read the headlines. On the same page, I highlighted Shivers Found Not Guilty in Blocking Budding Hoop Dreams.

"Wow," she said totally ignoring the article about the case we won. "I guess someone else will make the money – just like the Bernstein firm that represented the banker."

"The one who beat his wife into a coma," I asked.

"Yeah, he dropped like a quarter of a million dollars in his lawyer's lap," she replied.

Honestly, it would have been nice to snatch a paycheck like that, but I couldn't see me helping him avoid justice – especially, when he's done this before. I'd walk away from my practice before I represent his type.

As Audrey read the newspaper, I returned to my office to catch up on my own reading, while I surfed the Web for news. I glanced at the photograph of my grandmother across the room and couldn't help but think how much I missed her.

As a foster child, I found it extremely difficult to trust anyone. I never had a chance to meet my real parents. As far as I can remember and from what I was told, I was in the foster care system before I could sit up straight. Although I vaguely remember living with a few families, it was Ella Roberts, a foster parent who for years used her large home to provide shelter to countless unfortunate children, gave me a home and the love that saved my life.

I lived with Ms. Roberts, or grandma as I used to call her, since I was four. Sometimes, I get goose bumps thinking I've been living here for 30 years. She was already up in age, when I first moved in and always had other children living here. She was a good foster parent who cared for her children – not just putting on a show to collect monthly state checks. She always instilled the value of hard work, honesty and charity. Many kids who came to live with her, had real rough backgrounds; but over time, even they were able to get their life together and make it through the foster care system. Some even had the good fortune of adoption. I've seen a few of my foster siblings over the years, but I never maintained contact with any of them except for Audrey, who routinely came to visit grandma after she was adopted.

Out of the dozens of children grandma helped raise, I felt fortunate that she chose to adopt me before she retired. She never had any children of her own and rarely mentioned any members of her family, but she understood the importance of family nevertheless. Occasionally, grandma would try to get me to look through a box of old photographs and letters that belong to my biological parents, but I hated those pictures. I didn't want anything to do with them or form any false memories in my head. If they want me to know and remember them, they should be here, I thought. I remember her words clearly as we sat watching an episode of 'Diff'rent Strokes'.

"People ain't perfect," she'd say. "In order for a tree to bear fruit, it's got to know its roots."

I always felt like grandma was my Mr. Drummond – the way she sort of scooped me up into her big house and took me in. At 14, an age when I figured my chances for adoption looked slim, I made a decision that a good education would pave my way to success. One day as I sat at the dining room table doing my homework, Grandma came in to interrupt, while carrying Audrey in her arms.

"Erin, I need to talk to you," she called out.

"I don't want to see the pictures," I said okay, not really lifting my head from my albegra book. She pushed those pictures on me at least once a month.

"It's not that," she said. I sat my pencil down and looked at her. Perhaps she was going to tell me Audrey was leaving, or maybe ask for a hand in the kitchen or help going up the steps. She had started moving a little slower around the house and often asked for a hand here and there.

"I need you to know that you've always been my little angel," she said. She pulled up a seat next to me.

"I know grandma."

"No, sweetheart, I mean it more than just a nick name. Having you live here with me gives me a joy I've never had with my family or through the foster care program. I've already told you that I don't think I can keep providing care anymore with these tired old bones." Audrey, at two years old squirmed her way out of grandma's arms into my lap. "And they'll make me send you away if I give up what I do."

"That's okay grandma," I said. I gave Audrey a kiss and held her close. She and I had a quite special bond. "I only have a few more years. I'm sure I'll be okay living in another house."

"Heavens no, I'm not asking you to leave. I don't want you to go anywhere." She gently brushed my hair back from my forehead.

"But I thought you said that you are going to retire."

"I am, which is why I want to adopt you as my own," she said. "That is if it's okay with you."

I knew then what it felt like to have a prayer answered. There was nothing more special than that moment for me in all my life. I felt like I finally belonged to someone. I was wanted. I was loved. I cried in her arms for what seemed like the rest of the day. She cried along with me.

That evening, I took that box of photos and threw them in the trash out back.

"You don't have to do that," grandma said, while catching me in the act. "Those are still your parents."

"Don't need them. I have you now," I said. She walked over to me and placed her hand on my shoulder and we walked back inside.

Over the years, she and I had some good times and meaningful talks. When I needed a hug, she was there. When I needed the harsh truth, she was there for that too. The one thing grandma would always drop my way was encouragement. She'd say to me. "If you can believe, you can do anything. Erin, I taught you to believe, the rest is up to you." While she didn't open her home for foster care any longer, Grandma still found ways to give of herself. She volunteered through her church, gave to local charities, and was always willing to lend a hand.

We became a real family – Audrey included, though she was eventually adopted about eight years later. In our house there was laughter during sitcoms, church gossip, arguments about dating, and everything else. In middle school, when Kevin use to walk me home from school, Grandma always told me to be careful of that one. She said he reminded her of a stray cat. Be kind to him once and he'll never leave me alone. It wasn't until my senior year in college that Grandma's health began to really fade.

When I was accepted to Temple Law, I worried that I would lose her. And though we did have a few scares, she made it to my graduation. When she died, she left me this home. I miss her terribly, I thought to myself. What I would give to have another talk with her. I wouldn't even mind looking through that box of photographs with her.

As I reminisced about younger days, I was interrupted out of my thought by the sudden sound of the front door buzzer. It was a little after 10, and it was after a trial day, so I wasn't expecting any appointments.

I heard someone walking in and decided to step out of my office to see.

It was Kevin with a bag that smelled like breakfast.

"I come bearing food," he said. What a godsend, I thought. And here I was in my faded Temple Law hoodie and comfy jeans.

Faster than it took for him take off his coat, I grabbed the bag and Audrey and I inhaled every piece of food we could grab. For the next 20 minutes, the only sound in the entire office was the sound of a rummaged paper bag, mouth smacking and the sipping of coffee. I caught Kevin staring at me a few times and wondered what he thought about my grungy appearance.

"Okay, now that we've eaten breakfast, I need a favor," Kevin said, interrupting the comfortable silence.

"Favor? I should have known there was more to this than just a kind gesture," I said.

He held his hands out as if to say, hold on. "Hear me out."

I took a sip of my coffee.

"What do you want," I asked.

"I want you to spend the day with me."

"Huh?"

"Spend the day with me. I want to take you back to the firm to show you what we're all about."

"I know what you're about and I'm not interested Kevin."

"Come on Erin. What do you have to lose? At least take a look at the opportunity. Tell you what, you can bill me for the time," he said with his signature smile.

"What?"

"That's right. You can bill me as if I were a client." He paused. "A paying client."

Audrey jumped in. "You better take this fine man's offer, it's not like you have any appointments today."

I looked at Audrey hoping she'd mind her business or at least do some work.

"Look, let me show you around, introduce you to the partners and other staff and if you don't like what you see, go ahead and walk away from it. Just don't let me be a part of the story that you tell our kids in a few years about what you should have done."

The pressure grew and I buckled, finally rolling my eyes and nodding in agreement. "I just pray I don't regret this."

Kevin looked at his watch. "Great. Wanna get your coat? I know rush hour has already passed, but with all the construction downtown the lunch rush starts soon. We need to leave"

"Now?" I asked.

"What part of spend the day with me don't you understand?" Kevin started putting his coat on and pulled out his keys as if I had no choice.

"I guess the part that meant stop what you're doing," I said pointing to the pile of paper work and unopened mail in my office.

"Who are you trying to kid? You're not doing anything. You just finished a case," he said knowing my schedule a little too well.

"At least let me get dressed," I said referring to my garb.

"Yeah, you shouldn't go in wearing that," he teased. "Now if it said Howard Law, you'd be making a fashion statement."

CHAPTER 4

The council of angels listened intently as Jericho and Iblis argued before them.

"Council I am begging you, do not cast him out," Jericho pleaded. "We do not know what happened."

"That is not true," Iblis interrupted. "Aalon admits to killing him."

"Aalon admits he was at fault, but the intention was–"

"This is heaven!" Iblis yelled. "Sin is not accepted here. Aalon taints the purity that heaven demands. If you allow his blemish to stand, then others must be allowed entrance as well."

Aalon begged to be present for the argument, but was denied the opportunity to be among the council until his trial. Jericho knew how much he dreaded being cast out. He argued valiantly in Aalon's favor.

"If you let him go, Iblis will have his way with him and it is very possible he will fall," Jericho said calmly. "I am asking that you allow him to wait here through his trial.

"Fine," Iblis said. "Let him remain. I assure you, such favoritism will be recorded for eternity and I will see to it that all mankind knows heaven's rules bend for some.

"Enough!" the elder angel yelled. "Heaven's law never bends. I'm sorry Jericho, but Aalon cannot be held here."

Iblis turned to Jericho and smiled. "Thank you, wise council." He bowed in jest.

"Iblis, Aalon does not belong to you, he must be present for trial," said the same elder.

"I'll see to it personally," he said. He turned back to Jericho. "I'll send for him soon. See to it that he doesn't arrive late."

Iblis vanished into a cloud of darkness.

Jericho turned to the council and watched sadly as they walked out of the room one by one.

We pulled into the downtown parking garage of the Morris building, where the Hoffman Dudley Group's offices rented the top four floors. The building held more than two dozen businesses, including accounting firms, the administrative offices of the city's professional football team, an insurance company and more. It was one of the most impressive, well-secured and newest buildings downtown. Kevin's parking spot was less than 10 spaces away from the garage's elevator, his name firmly plated on the wall to let others know the spot belonged to him.

"Kevin, this may not be such a good idea after all," I said breaking the silence. I just realized how much the corporate setting turned me off. "I hate to put you through all this trouble only to --"

"We're here now, let me just show you around, introduce you to a few people, that's all." He said. I must admit, his smoothness made it a little harder for me to keep the wall up. "If you don't like what you see, you can let it go and I'll let it go."

I didn't respond. He had already unlocked the door and stepped out to come over to my side to open the door for me. He was such a gentleman.

When we stepped inside the elevator, looking out I could see all the expensive luxury and sports cars lined up with Kevin's new Massarati keeping up with the pack. Sure made my little Volkswagen a certified clunker.

We made it to the lobby elevator where he swiped his key and pushed the number 22. Surprisingly, the elevator didn't stop once.

"This is a bypass key. When I swipe, no one on any other floor can interrupt my trip, he said over the elevator tune "Baby its cold outside." He smiled, kissed the key and placed it back in his inside pocket.

Less than a minute later, we stepped into the partner suite – an entire floor of luxury offices. The expensive Mahogany wood trim, gorgeous hardwood floors, antique paintings and decorative lighting could certainly have competed with anything offered in the finest of museums or mansions.

"Closest thing to heaven you'll see in a long time, huh?" he said as he took my coat and handed it to the receptionist. "Let's take a look around."

EVEN *Angels* NEED MIRACLES

CHAPTER 5

In between exploring her Facebook account, Audrey stayed glued to her laptop researching contact information for some of the cases Erin requested earlier. She walked into Erin's office and placed a handwritten message concerning Antonio Walker on her desk. Someone called earlier looking for representation. When she came back to her desk, a woman was standing in the lobby, which startled her.

"Was the door unlocked?" Audrey asked. No one was able to get in without the buzzer.

"I'm sorry, if I startled you," the woman said. "I'm here to see Erin. Is she in?"

"She is not here at the moment, but I can set an appointment for you if you'd like.

"This is kind of an emergency. When will she return?"

"What's the nature of the emergency?" Audrey asked, not that she could get her back any sooner, but she was curious as to whether or not this was someone who wanted free representation. Audrey did her best to protect her sister from those that would take advantage of her kindness. "I can call her. What's this about?"

"It's a matter of extreme importance. I'm sorry, but I am not permitted to share with you. I have to speak to Erin."

Audrey was just a tad offended that the woman didn't give her any more information. She didn't bother to offer any more help than the minimum.

"Well, she's out at a meeting at this time. I can make sure she calls you when she gets back. What's your name?"

"Sleep" the woman said gently. She didn't know if her ability had left her.

"What was that?"

"Sleep." She said a little louder.

Audrey was out cold. If it hadn't been for her gel-filled wrist pad placed at the edge of her desk, she would have banged her head with enough force to leave a nasty bruise. Athyna breathed a sigh of relief. She would have felt extremely guilty had this woman injured herself. As she leaned Audrey back in her chair and rolled it a foot or two away from the desk, the front door buzzed. Athyna looked up to see a tiny little woman standing out front. She scrolled through Erin's calendar on her laptop and checked the clock.

Yvonne's name was written.

"Sorry Yvonne if that's you," Athyna whispered. She looked down on the desk and saw an envelope marked 'Yvonne's key.'

She continued to look through Audrey's schedule for more information on Erin.

"Out for the day," she whispered to herself.

The ring of the phone startled her. She looked at the caller ID and saw it was Erin.

Athyna wrote down the number and let the voicemail answer the call.

She tried not to move too much until Yvonne was gone. She saw her trying to get a peek inside and hoped she didn't see anything. As Yvonne walked off, Athyna adjusted the laptop so that it was back to Audrey's original screen and slid her chair back to her desk. She felt bad about not answering the door and decided to make sure Yvonne made it safely to where she needed to go. She didn't know what she would do if something bad happened to her or anyone else because of her interference. That's the risk with coming on an unofficial or unauthorized mission. She took the envelope with Yvonne's key and left. Who knew how important that key was to her? Just as the door clicked behind Athyna, Audrey woke up without any memory of the visit, although she had a terrible headache.

"Hi sister," said the receptionist as she entered the hospital. Sister Mary smiled pleasantly and walked through. She was a little later than normal for her room visits. She spent another long period in confession.

As she waited for the elevator in silence, she pondered at the priest's implore only moments ago.

"Sister Mary, you must let the past go. You were a mere child yourself," he pleaded.

"Father I try," she cried. "But when I see these young women, who I try to help. It reminds me of the pain. It stirs up such sore memories. "Maybe God is telling me I have no business trying to serve him."

"Sister I assure you God holds nothing against you," the priest, wished he could console her. Sister Mary now at almost 65 years old has held on to her hurt for more than 40 years. He has assigned her more Our Fathers and Hail Mary's than any other confessor. It was obvious, what she needed he couldn't provide. "Monica, is with God now," he whispered.

"Do not say her name! Father, please. Do not say her name!"

"Sister are you getting on?" The gentleman on the elevator and the few others behind him waited patiently. They were almost a bit embarrassed to interrupt her deep thought.

"Oh, yes," she said kindly. "She pulled out a handkerchief to wipe her tears and stepped on board. "Don't ever get as old as me." She turned to the group. They all had a good laugh.

CHAPTER 6

"You'd love it here," Kevin said. "I've been here four years and already, they're talking about making me a partner. "What more could I ask for?"

A knock on Kevin's door interrupted

"Good morning Kevin," said the woman. Behind her walked in an older man, who took a few steps and stood in front of his desk. Kevin stood up to shake his hand.

"Mr. Dudley," he said. "What brings you by?" David Dudley was co-founder of the Dudley Hoffman Firm. At 60 years old he was considered one of Baltimore's most successful and perhaps most wealthy lawyers in the entire state. His firm rivaled even some of the larger Manhattan firms in terms of assets and prestige. He was a living achievement.

"I wanted to meet Erin for myself," he said. He turned to me to shake my hand. "Oh don't get up. Sit down, sit down."

I sat as he walked over to shake my hand. His grip was very firm as if he were sealing a deal. It was obvious he stayed in good shape. He could certainly pass for a man in his mid-forties.

"Did you show her around Kevin?" He asked.

"I did. I was just telling her how much she would like it here."

"Great, great. Well, I don't want to hold you two up. But please if you have any questions, Kevin should be able to help you. If not, please feel free to call me direct." The woman handed me a business card. "Kevin, keep up the fine work."

Within a few seconds they were gone.

"What is it that you think you couldn't get from this firm?" Kevin asked.

"Oh I don't know, a clean conscience maybe. An honest reputation."

"You don't quit do you?" Kevin asked smiling. "I'll admit, we have some less than perfect clients, but I keep away from anything that I find suspect and I do my job honestly. With all the victories under my belt, I must be doing something right."

"But that's just it Kevin. If this firm goes down, then you go down. Oh and you can decrease all your wins by one, if you count our mock trial I beat you in high school."

"You still haven't let that go," he said jokingly.

"That's only because you haven't."

Kevin looked at his lap top and performed a few clicks on the mouse, then closed it.

I looked at the text message on my phone from Audrey.

Antonio Walker's people called... interested?

Not a chance I responded. *Busy.*

I put away the phone as Kevin turned his attention to me. "So changing the subject briefly, you think it's not okay to represent someone that's committed a crime?"

"No I never said that! Everyone deserves equal representation and due process under the law. I just don't think a lawyer should argue that the defendant didn't commit a crime when they know they did it."

"Define know," Kevin said. "I mean, who are we to say our client committed a crime. If my client tells me he didn't do it. That's all I need to know."

"You mean that's all you want to know," I said. I couldn't help but notice how plush his office was. I got up from my chair to get a closer look at what must serve as his wall of fame. Several plaques and photographs adorned nicely. There were photos of him with public officials, sports celebrities and a few golf photos with the guys. "I don't want a client that only tells me what they need to in order to appear innocent. Either be completely honest with me and tell me everything or find another lawyer."

Kevin walked over to adjust a plaque that was a little off center. He turned to me.

"As a lawyer, it's my job to give my client the best possible service. So if that means advising him not to tell me certain things, that's what I'm going to do. I'm not supposed to judge him. That's for the jury."

Another knock at his door.

"Come in," he said.

"Sorry to bother you Mr. Banneker, I have a file for you. Looks like you landed the Antonio Walker case."

She handed him the folder. He took a quick peek at the materials inside. "Just continue to think about it. You know, let it marinate. You could land high profile cases such as this one."

"Right," I said. "I probably could."

"Okay, enough with the chit chat. Let's go grab some lunch." Kevin stood up. With one hand, he held on to the Walker file, with the other, he extended his hand to help me out my chair.

I spent the next two and a half hours talking and listening to Kevin about his position and the firm. We managed to also discuss politics, religion, growing up, sports and other non-important stuff. It might have been an official date if we could find something to agree on. The lunch ended nicely though. After all, Kevin was known for his charm. I can't say he didn't didn't impress me. We spent a little time cruising around the city and talking. Before too long, daylight started to end.

She didn't know why this night felt so strange, but clearly there was something different about this evening. It was a little past seven p.m. and already it was pretty dark. Yvonne walked out of the church from rehersal. As usual, she was the last to leave. After locking up and walking a few steps, she made her way down the dark alley. Normally, there was a street light hanging from the adjacent building's side that would light the path, but tonight it was out. "Father get me through this alley," she whispered. Though she's walked through it countless nights before, she felt a bit different about this time. She just wanted to make it home. She hoped someone would be in the law office when she got back, since she still didn't have a working key.

"Give up the bag lady," said the young man as he came from behind the dumpster and shoved her into the wall.

Before she could scream, another man grabbed her and cupped her mouth. She let go of her purse as instructed.

"We got the bag. Let's go," said the one who gave her the huge shove from behind.

"Wait a minute, lets have a little fun," his hand stayed around her mouth as his other hand started to make its way from her waist to her breast.

"Come on man! Let's get out of here."

"Hold on! I'm not done yet. Put the pistol on her."

Just like a nervous yes man, he pulled the gun from his coat pocket and aimed it at Yvonne.

Yvonne closed her eyes and began to cry. "Please," she said through his hand.

It was a Tuesday night, and to her it seemed as if no one existed in the world, except for the three. Not a pedestrian or car crossed their location. If only someone would walk by.

Athyna turned down the alley, and saw the struggle. She followed Yvonne, since she left Erin's building and patiently waited for her to finish work and complete her errands. As Yvonne prayed for safety in the alley. Athyna could sense her fear. Though she remembered Jericho's warning to be careful and that she could be hurt, she couldn't let this occur. Especially sense she felt partly responsible for seeing that Yvonne made it home safely tonght. Hopefully, she'd be all right.

"Get out of here woman!" yelled the fondler.

She continued to walk toward them.

"Seriously lady. Beat it, unless you want a hot one in you," the gun carrier turned the gun onto Athyna,

"I'm through playing with both of these women," said the fondler. "He pushed Yvonne to the ground and walked toward Athyna. He swung to hit her only to have her catch his fist in the air and sling him by the arm into the brick wall, knocking him out cold. The other guy shot the gun. Yvonne screamed and pulled out her cell phone to call the police. Two bullets hit Athyna. One ricocheted and hit the brick wall in front of her. She grabbed him by his coat and slung him into the dumpster. He too, was unconscious and ended up laying on top of his associate.

"My God," Yvonne said hysterically. "You're hurt, you must be hurt."

"I'm okay," Athyna said. She used her hands to check her body. She didn't feel injured, but she did feel a small notch in her side and noticed one of the bullets embedded. It was in pretty deep. Thank goodness there was no pain – at least not yet.

"Let me help you," Yvonne said. My church is right there. Please."

"Yvonne, I'm okay. If you want to help, go home. This is for you. She handed her a small envelope with her name on it. It contained her key. Tell her, its in the red tool box in the attic."

"Tell who, what red tool box."

Athyna laid down and closed her eyes. The sound of sirens went by.

"I'll get help. Just hold on," Yvonne said.

Yvonne ran down the alley screaming. She turned the corner to wave down the police car that was obviously in the area responding to the gun shots. The police rolled the side window down.

"There's a woman in the alley. She helped me and she's hurt. Hurry!" She ran back as the squad car hit a U-Turn. When she got to the alley, Athyna was gone – no trail of blood or any other sign to show she'd even been there. The two assailants, however, laid there still out cold.

After Kevin pulled near the curb, he opened my door and walked me to my front door. I could vaguely hear Yvonne playing and singing, with more passion and exuberance than I've heard in quite a while. Already, it began to put me at ease. Kevin softly took hold of my hand and escorted me to my door. "I'm not asking you to go against your principles. Everyone who works for this firm is not bad. I just think you would do well here." He let go of my hand and gave me a kiss on the cheek as he made his way back to the car. "The firm wants you Erin. Why not be that person that changes the things you don't like about Hoffman and Dudley?"

"It's not mine to change," I said.

"Sleep on it and I'll accept whatever answer you have tomorrow." He got in his car and drove away.

I unlocked the door and stepped in. The first message that was posted on the wall for me to see read Antonio Walker received representation by Hoffman and Dudley.

"I was there," I said with a slight chuckle. I kicked off my shoes and carried them in my hand. It was almost 8 p.m. and Audrey was gone. No sooner than I started making my way to my apartment than I heard a knock at the door behind me. On instinct I opened the door thinking it was Kevin.

Surprisingly, the woman I met earlier was standing there.

"Sorry, but the office is closed," I said not really appreciating her total intrusion.

"I just want to talk with you."

"I'd really prefer that we talked during my business hours," I said, politely but assertively. I started to push the door close. The woman stuck her hand in the way.

"Erin, please this is of extreme importance. There is no need to fear me. Please allow me to come in and just talk with you."

I sensed a level of urgency with this woman unlike ever before. I could tell she had a story to share and I couldn't resist my own inquisitiveness. Despite thinking it better to wait until the morning, I let her into my home.

CHAPTER 7

"Aalon, it is time," the messenger angel said as he opened the door to the holding room as two hooded fallens walked in to place restraints on him. While demons always show their true gruesome form in heaven, the fallens that were lucky enough to return to heaven with messages or on a mission for Iblis, usually wore hoods. They were rightfully ashamed of the choices they made which lead to their banishment and wished not to be recognized. Most fallen angels remember vividly their life in heaven and regret their banishment. The peace, camaraderie and love that flowed from heart to heart become instantly replaced with pain, distrust and hate. And while every fallen (except the first) would give anything to return to heaven, their fear of Iblis' wrath motivated them to complete the task he assigned them without question or second thoughts. Iblis often teased his recruited angels with the idea of returning, but never delivered. Plenty of angels tried to re-enter only to receive the immortal torture – an eternal existence of nonstop suffering.

"Aalon no longer enjoys your protection. You WILL NOT talk with him."

Yoseph, Aalon's escort, approached the fallen with anger-filled eyes.

"As long as he stands in this compound, he is under my protection. And you two will abide by the rules of THIS house!"

The fallens looked at the seriousness in Yoseph and knew it was only a matter of time before Aalon and the two of them were outside the hold, heaven's makeshift detainment facility, which served primarily as a waiting room/study for the high ranking angels and direct reports to the Almighty. Messenger, healing, archangels, archons, cherubims, seraphims and several more types of angels often visited the room for uninterrupted thinking and planning. Guardians, especially used the room to prepare life reports for the angelic council. The life reports contained every minute detail of an assignment's life from the very number of hairs on his head to the thoughts in his mind and the decisions made throughout a given lifetime. Since learning the news of Aalon, it was decided to keep him there until his departure.

"You are moving too slow!" One of the fallens said referring to Yoseph's pace. The two fallens were anxious to receive full possession and control. "I will give a full report of this resistance immediately!"

"What resistance? I am escorting him to the gates as promised," Yoseph said. In his heart he would admit to delaying the inevitable, but he'd never admit it to them.

"Let them move slowly," said the shorter fallens. "We will move slowly when we have our way with him."

Aalon closed his eyes in a desperate attempt to reach HIS Mercy, but he felt nothing.

Yoseph sadly placed a hand on Aalon's shoulder. "HE will not hear you."

"Where is Athyna?" Aalon asked. "She promised to see me." Athyna and Aalon were close and held a bond much like brother and sister; and while all angels were seen as one family under God, some angels were closer to others, like in any other family. Athyna and Aalon were that way.

"I've not spoken to her. All I know is she and Jericho are working in your favor."

A long pause took place, before Aalon spoke quietly to Yoseph as they approached the gate.

Yoseph found it extremely difficult to look Aalon in the eye. He knew that

The Dark One and those in the dark world would do their best to tempt Aalon to fall and succumb to the ways of the flesh and to purposely set out to fulfill his own desires. A true test awaited Aalon, a test that humans have struggled with and angels have yet to experience – a test of faith.

Yoseph embraced his brother. "I cannot lie to you Aalon," he said. "You will be tempted, but if I had to put belief in one that could resist, I believe you can. I believe you will return. I believe the works are already taken place."

Almost since the beginning of time, man has been faced with fleshly temptation and more often than not man falls. On Earth, The Dark One has his limitations on what he can do, but in his world, on his terms, there's not been any to overcome the temptation or torment. During Aalon's stay, while undergoing trial, he was open to just about every tactic The Dark One could conspire, with the exception of the immortal torture. If he was broken to fall, the trial wouldn't matter. He would spend his eternity in hell serving Iblis. Yoseph opened the gate just as instructed. Aalon turned to take one final look at Yoseph. He started to fill with fear and uncertainty.

Before a final goodbye the two fallens snatched him into the darkest scream-filled shadow ever created.

CHAPTER 8

The young child slid out of Sister Mary's arms and climbed into bed. A faint giggle escaped from his mother. Sister Mary stood up from the rocking chair in the corner of the room. It was nearing 9:30 and she felt a bit guilty holding the toddler up past his bed time. She walked to the door that led to the hall. She motioned for the boy's mother to follow.

"What are your plans?" Sister Mary asked. The two had spoken the last hour or so about the turmoil that has grown in her home. They didn't want to talk too much about Jason, her boyfriend, with her son in the room.

"I'm going back to Charlotte," she said. My brother lives there and he said we can live with him – at least until I get on my feet."

"Sounds good," Sister Mary said. She was glad Samantha was getting out of Jason's reach and the fact that she would be living with her brother made her feel even more comfortable. "Do you have money, for travel?"

"I have a little. It will probably take me a few weeks to earn enough for me and Bryce."

"Take this. This will get you both there sooner," Sister Mary reached into her habit and pulled out an envelope. Samantha teared up again. She just couldn't believe how gracious Sister Mary was.

"I promise I'll pay you back as soon as I am able."

"Just promise you'll at least call once you're there safe," she said. They hugged for almost a full minute. "Samantha please use this money to get you and your son to your brother's. Do not wait until it's too late to make the change."

Samantha stared at Sister Mary. She was determined to make good on this promise. "Sister, you have my word. Bryce and I will be on a plane to Charlotte by the weekend." Sister Mary's heart felt much lighter. "Thank you again." They hugged one last time, before Sister Mary made her way down the hall.

"I'm not crazy." The woman said sitting down in front of my desk. She appeared to be grimacing in pain. "I'm an angel."

I honestly tried to sit and listen, but I couldn't contain my annoyance. I can't believe I let this strange woman in my house and gave this much attention to her nonsense. I replayed my day in my head and decided I messed up at accepting Kevin's invitation this morning. Had I just stuck to my regular routine, I would have already found myself cozying up to my favorite book in front of the fireplace or watching a movie with a glass of wine and her buzzing or knocking would have gone ignored. I desperately hoped she would say what she had to and leave, but she just paused after telling me she was an angel again as if I were going to take the bait. I tried to force myself to fake interest, but decided I'd had enough. I wanted to enjoy the rest of my off-day evening.

"You know what? I'm going to have to ask that you leave," I said. "I don't mean to cut you off, but I've had a long day. I'm tired and really want to catch up on some rest." There, I tried honesty, I thought.

I stood up from behind the desk to gesture the meeting was over.

"I'm telling you the truth," she said.

"Look, umm…I'm sorry I never got your name,"

"Athyna," she said as she started to close her eyes, I couldn't tell if she was sleeping, praying, or just high on drugs. Whatever the case, my patience was thin.

"Okay Athyna, I'm going to ask once more, very nicely, would you please leave? Maybe we can talk tomorrow."

She just sat sluggishly as if my request didn't register. She appeared to drift in and out of consciousness

"Actually forget I said that." I reached for the phone and pressed 911. They were pretty quick in answering. "Yes, I have someone in my home, who I've asked to leave and she is refusing. Could you please send a police officer to assist me? She may also need help if you know what I mean. Hold on, I'll ask. Athyna, are you armed? You carrying any weapons?"

Athyna shook her head. She winced in pain with every movement.

"No she's unarmed," I said while staring at the clock. I gave them my address and hung up.

"How long do I have," she asked, surprisingly very calmly.

"They say someone will be here in less than five minutes."

"Well, then I guess I'll take my chances and talk until they come," she said. "If that's okay with you?"

I couldn't believe she decided to wait. She's either crazier than I thought or perhaps she thought I was bluffing.

"Hey, it's your night, if you want to spend it in jail, that's up to you."

"Erin, I'm an angel of the Lord. I've come not to hurt, deceive, or confuse you but to ask for your help." She paused and closed her eyes again.

"Are you all right?" I asked. It was obvious she was struggling with the effects of an injury, drugs or something.

"I should be okay," she said "Listen, a great unwritten tragedy has occurred. Actually, it is occurring and I've come to seek your help in the matter."

Athyna barely managed to stand up and walk toward me. I stepped back but she was able to touch my hand, giving off a sensation that seemed to warm my heart. I pulled my hand back and was relieved to hear the knock on the door. I could see from the window the red and blue lights flashing from the street.

"There's your ride," I made my way to the door, walking quickly to end this bizarre encounter.

"Erin, you are a believer. I know that. This may all be strange to you, but you're not the kind of person who doesn't at least hear the story." Athyna stared at me with a look so convincing, it was scary. Her eyes fixated on mine as if she were trying to speak to something deeper inside me. "Please hear me. You can save his life. Please," she begged.

I fought my instinct to hear her out as I turned the door knob to let the police in.

"Hello ma'am. We got a call about an intruder," the officer said as he instantly looked past me to see Athyna. "Is this her?"

I opened the door wider and motioned for him to come inside but I didn't answer. The officer briskly walked toward Athyna, while muttering a series of coded numbers in the radio attached to his torso.

"Ma'am, you need to come with us," he said as he gently grabbed Athyna's hand.

When she pulled away from him, he became more aggressive and forced her hand behind her back and pushed her into the wall to cuff her.

"Hey, not so rough," I chimed in.

"Ma'am please step back. I can handle this." Athyna pushed off the wall with her foot causing the officer to lose his balance. She walked toward me. Her strength began to fade even more before my eyes.

"Erin!" she yelled. With one solid motion, the officer wrestled Athyna to the ground as a second officer who saw the commotion from the front door ran inside to assist him. "If you don't believe, you can't help. Look for the red–" She drifted to sleep.

Yvonne's music seemed to suddenly stop. She probably was bothered by all the noise.

The cops walked her outside to the squad car. I wanted to make sure she was going to be okay. She looked totally limp when they placed her in the back seat. Her head rested against the window.

"She'll be okay ma'am," the officer said as a response to my look of concern. "She's probably on that stuff. We'll give her a place to sleep it off."

"Don't you think she should go to the hospital," I asked.

"We go through at least a dozen of these a night. She'll be okay. Trust me. You did the right thing by calling us." The police handed me a brief report of the evening, which I signed and before you know it, he and his partner were in the car with the engine started. Yvonne came outside, to see what all the fuss was about. She squinted her eyes at the car.

"STOP!" she yelled, but the police car pulled off. "That's her! That's her!"

I walked over to Yvonne.

"Do you know her?" I asked. It was freezing outside. My words came out in almost a stammering fashion.

"Yes," she said. She blew into her hands. The robe she was wearing was nowhere near thick enough to protect her from the bitter chill. "I mean not really. She helped me earlier today."

"What do you mean," I asked. The police car faded out of site. Yvonne closed her eyes and started whispering. She seemed to be thinking out loud. "Red toolbox in the attic."

"What?"

"Do you have a red toolbox in the attic?"

EVEN *Angels* NEED MIRACLES

CHAPTER 9

"Master he's here." Geragan, the tall, muscular fallen, said in his deep voice as he led the bound Aalon into the archway. Geragan was Iblis' personal servant. His scowl intimidated everyone except Iblis. As a former lieutenant in the angelic army, he was Jericho's protégé. He was a master at spiritual combat and always anxious to take down an angel – especially since they refused to forgive his actions, which led him to hell. Aalon's capture was a blessing in his opinion. He could barely contain his excitement and wanted to get started with his revenge.

"Leave us," Iblis said as he waved Geragan away. Iblis, in what looked like a customized hooded suit, bent down. His slender fingers wrapped themselves around the chain connected to Aalon's neck and wrists and gently tugged, pulling him slowly to the center of the floor. Then, surprisingly, he separated the chains and locks.

As Aalon rubbed his wrists and neck, Iblis stared at Aalon for what seemed like an eternity. His gruesome smile was enough to send chills down any spine.

"I told you they didn't have tolerance for imperfection," he said in a most belittling manner. "Are you afraid?" He softly asked as he bent lower to pick up the chains. He held them up without looking at them and a fallen came in to relieve him from holding them and just as quickly walked out of the room. "Are you afraid?" He asked again.

Aalon hesitated to answer, "I don't know."

"You've been here only a short while and you're avoiding truth already." He said while carrying that same smile. "That happens easily here. But Aalon, there is no need to fear me. I'm not interested in harming you." Iblis walked toward the mirror and adjusted his collar. He brushed off his chest and shoulders as if dust had managed to cling to the surface of his jacket. He appeared calm and confident.

"Then why am I here?"

"Something about the murder, perhaps." Iblis laughed, while still staring in the mirror. He turned toward Aalon and waved a finger. "Don't forget, your divine angelic council sent you. Not me. The council, despite their wanting to allow you to stay with them, felt in order to preserve heaven's integrity, it would serve best if you remained outside the gates."

"Only because you've raised false charges," Aalon responded. His anger visibly showing, but still reserved.

"Me, raise false charges?" Iblis placed his hands on his chest to gesture his hurt by the accusation. Walking closer to Aalon, he jabbed a finger in his chest, pushing him back slightly. "But yet, you're here."

"It's temporary," Aalon said. His balance began to shake at the push of Iblis. Just before he stumbled, Iblis grabbed his arm to sturdy him.

"I too believed that Aalon – ahh, yes millenniums ago." Iblis said with a sigh. "But, I call it home now. Enough with our talk. I've much to do. Allow me to have someone escort you to your quarters. We have time for more discussion later."

Aalon didn't know what to think. His quarters? From what he thought and heard, he expected immediate torture, punishment and other forms of anguish. Perhaps this was all a test or trap.

As Aalon followed his escort, he turned back to face Iblis. He didn't feel comfortable having his back exposed to the Prince of Darkness. He determined in his mind, he would not fall.

With a tiny bell he pulled from his lapel pocket, Iblis summoned Geragan immediately after Aalon was out of sight.

"Yes Master," Geragan said abruptly. Traces of smoke still hovered over him as he appeared almost magically.

"See to it that he is given the best of care."

"Best of care?" Geragan looked dumbfounded.

Iblis tilted his head in surprise. "Must I repeat myself?" He questioned angrily. "If any harm comes to him, I will hold you personally responsible."

"I will see that Aalon receives the best of care." Geragan repeated in a military fashion. Though his face showed total confusion, he knew better than to ask for clarity or why. He bowed his head faithfully and left the same way he entered in a puff of dark smoke. Iblis stood by himself with an evil scowl. His wife entered quietly.

"I take it something is working in your thoughts. You confuse even me my Lord," Delilah said as she came to Iblis' backside and hugged him. "You allow Aalon to go unchained? He has a room in your finest quarters?"

"All with good measure my precious," Ibis said while turning to face his wife. He grabbed her by the jaw line to lift her mouth to his. He tightened his grip. If she had bones, they would have snapped. He loved hearing her soft wince in pain and over time, she grew to love it as well. "Nothing weakens an enemy more than trust."

Delilah knew this all too well. She could still vividly remember how she captured men's secrets, sanity and souls through the disguise of trust and love. Though it would mean torment for her if Iblis ever found out, she sometimes wondered if the same could be done to him.

CHAPTER 10

Kevin pulled the attic door down. "Tell me you didn't call me over at 11:00 to get something out of the attic for you. His slippers didn't want to hold him steady on the ladder.

"I just need you to check up there for a red tool box," I answered as he climbed the folding ladder.

"It's colder than outside up here," he said back. Plus there's no light. I can't see anything. Can't this wait until the morning?"

Yvonne and I answered in unison, "NO!"

"Here use this," Yvonne said while passing up her cellphone to him. She activated a light mode which shone from the back, near the camera.

He took it and was in the attic moving around.

"You have a lot of junk up here."

"I know its from the foster kids that lived here," I called back.

"You said a red tool box?"

"Yes," again Yvonne and I yelled together.

"I think I see it, hold on." Kevin rummaged around a few minutes and stired up some dust around the entry. I could hear him sliding something heavy above us. "Got it! I'm coming down and its heavy so back away."

When we sat down the dusty toolbox, we all noticed the pad lock on the front.

"Okay so what's so important about your tool box tonight," he asked sarcastically. "Do you have a few screws lose somewhere?" He laughed to himself.

I just stared at the box. I've been in the attic on many occassions and I'm sure I've seen this box a few times. I never thought to look inside though – just didn't' seem important.

"Whatever is in this box Erin, Kevin and I don't need to see it," Yvonne said.

I turned to her surprisingly.

"I don't mind," I said.

"It's not for us to know. That, I'm sure of," Yvonne said.

"Wait a minute, I want to see what's in this thing," Kevin said. "Especially if I had to leave my house at eleven o'clock to go up there and get it. It was cold up there." He folded up the ladder and pushed the attic door closed.

"It's locked anyway," Yvonne said.

"Wait," I said. Lets take it downstairs."

Kevin carried it down to the main floor. We both followed. I walked into my office and grabbed a hammer to beat the lock off. Just as I pulled it back over my shoulders with both hands, Kevin grabbed it from me.

"Give me that before you hurt yourself," Kevin said. He took the hammer. This lock looks a bit frail. Do you have a solid screw driver?"

I shook my head.

"Aww forget it." He lifted the hammer and banged on the lock one good time and it popped open. "Alright, first try."

"That's our que to leave," Yvonne said. She grabbed Kevin's arm and guided him to the door. "Come on, you can walk me around the corner and make sure I make it home safe."

"You gotta be kidding me," Kevin questioned.

"Maybe Yvonne is right?" I said. "I'm sorry. Thanks for your help. Both of you."

I walked them out the door and locked it before slowly walking back to the tool box. I wondered what this was all about as I knelt down and opened it.

CHAPTER 11

"Is he gone?"

"Yes," Jericho said as he recorded the new entry in the Dark book, the book that listed every soul that refused to believe. Sean made his eternal bed in hell and next to his name he wrote the name Aalon. All souls have their guardian's name next to theirs. "He left just a while ago." Jericho's response seemed short, almost like he didn't want to talk about Aalon's departure.

"I didn't think the Light would allow-"

Jericho closed the book loudly as he interrupted the young servant angel Salgiel. Though angels were all created at the same time at the calling of the Lord, they were each just as unique as humans. They looked differently. They had different personalities. They learned at different paces and had different levels of maturity. They also varied in knowledge and capacities for understanding. Salgiel equated to what an adolescent human or teenager would rank – knew everything, quick to speak, and un-recognizing of the little experience he truly possessed.

"The Light does not bend the rules for our pleasure or for anyone else's."

"He bends them for the Earth world all the time."

"HE does not bend the rules!" Jericho said. He stepped forward quickly and stood face to face with Salgiel. "Do not let me hear you repeat that." Salgiel didn't know if Jericho would strike him or do something even more out of nature. He stepped back and softened his tone.

"Then tell me why they are allowed entry with records of lies, stealing and even murders."

Obviously Salgiel referred to the mercy granted to humans. Such talk rarely surfaced in the open, but served as common talking points among angels in secret, particularly the younger natured ones.

"Even with your limited knowledge, surely, you know about HIS grace. You know that the Light's love allows cleansing. So there are no records, as you say, for those aggressions." Jericho pulled another book from his shelf. The Book of Life. The book that listed all souls who chose to believe. Though sometimes their life actions proved questionable, the hearts were right with God. "All of the humans are here because of HIS grace."

"Where is HIS grace for us?"

"Enough!."

"Where is HIS Grace for Aalon?"

"Get Out Now!" Jericho clutched the spine of the book. He did all he could not to throw it, but he too needed answers, much like Salgiel and many others. He did not want to see Aalon fall.

Salgiel turned and walked out of the library.

Jericho began to pray and decided on his next move – an unthinkable sacrifice.

CHAPTER 12

Aalon discovered the truth about trying to communicate with heaven from his quarters. He tried praying, talking and even thinking about the Light, only to find that his efforts felt futile. There existed a lack of closeness – the likes of which he's never experienced. He clasped his hands and closed his eyes in earnest. He angrily stood up from his desk and fell to his knees.

"Please hear me father," he started.

"That's a wasted prayer," Delilah said as she leaned with her arms folded in the door way. Aalon stood up as if on guard. Delilah gave a half smile and softened her eyes. She looked enticing, but her beauty proved deadly.

"Relax, Delilah at your service," she said while stepping in from the hall. "I thought you might be hungry. I brought you –"

"I know who you are and I'm not hungry." He answered. "Please leave." Aalon stared at Delilah with such an un-inviting look that she froze in mid-sentence."

"Well, let me know if you need anything," she said. "She plucked a grape from the bunch she bought and popped one in her mouth. She walked near him and lightly guided her finger from hhis shoulder to his wrist. "If you do not wish to eat, can I bring you something else?"

"No," he replied quickly.

She backed away slowly as if to let her sultry energy linger. Just as she started to leave, Aalon broke the silence.

"No wait!" He said. "A scroll."

"A what?" she asked.

"You can bring me a scroll."

Aalon felt he needed a word from on high. While his prayers felt empty, he figured he'd read the holy scrolls – the angel version of what man knows as the Bible – the pure, complete text of God's word. The Bible, no matter the version held only about 60 percent of what the scrolls contained.

"Oh. Sure, one of those," Delilah said in disgust. She rolled her eyes and pointed to the shelf on the back wall. "Really, there is no reward here for your efforts, but check on the shelf across from your bed if you must."

CHAPTER 13

Tools at the bottom, but more than a hundred photographs and letters from my parents flooded the top half of red tool box. I felt overwhelmed with emotion. There was one envelope with the words "My Angel" written across it in grandma's hand writing. I opened it slowly.

Dear Erin,

I'm not sure when you will get around to reading this, but I couldn't let you toss your family away like that. I know you get upset sometimes about your situation, but its because of of your parent's imperfections we found each other. I know this might sound selfish, but I love you too much to wish for another outcome. Your parents couldn't have been all that bad to make a darling little angel like yourself. Please hold on to this box. I got a strong feeling if you throw this away again, I won't be able to get it back for you. I love you always. Grandma.

I spent the next hour looking at pictures, reading dates and names on the back and wiping the tears from my eyes. Just today I was thinking how much I would love to spend time with gradma doing this exact thing and here I was just about doing it.

I called Kevin and Yvonne and told them about the contents of the toolbox. I told them I was okay and once again thanked them for their assistance. After hanging up and setting the box to the side, Athyna popped into my mind. How did she know? I'd make sure to find out in the morning.

Sister Harriet was certain Sister Mary was crying – again. It was late into the night and she could see her light was on from the bottom of her door frame in her room. It seems this was her routine every night.

"I pray Father, you'll give her rest. Whatever she is struggling with, help her to release it," she whispered. She stood outside of Sister Mary's closed door, kissed her rosary as she stared at Sister Mary's room and continued to walk her rounds in the building.

In the room, sister Mary laid curled in bed holding on to her framed picture. Her tear-soaked pillow finally allowed her to sleep.

It was 9:00 on the nose when the officer walked me back to the holding cell. I would have come sooner, but their processing center wouldn't allow me to post bail until moments ago. Athyna laid against the wall by herself almost lifeless. It was only a few degrees warmer than outside, which is probably why she was huddled in her coat.

"Let's go," the officer bellowed. "You've made bail."

"My God! Why wasn't she taken to a hospital?" I asked. "Look at her."

It was hard to believe but she looked even worse than last night. She was pale and appeared almost lifeless. I walked in and helped her to her feet.

She barely opened her eyes and smiled.

"You came for me," she whispered with a smile.

"Come on, we need to talk," I said. "But first you need to go to the hospital."

I helped her to her feet, which seemed to put her in a little pain. She seemed warm to the touch, like she had a high fever.

"Jericho can help me," she said before releasing a soft cough. I had no idea what she was talking about. To be quite frank, I didn't care. Though, I wanted to know how she knew my grandmother and about the toolbox, I really did want to see her get better and knew she needed medical attention. We made our way out of the cell and the building. The officer provided no assistance. We managed to make it to my car, where I helped to buckle her into the back seat. She needed immediate attention.

"Thank you," she mumbled.

I adjusted the rearview mirror so I could see Athyna who sort of slumped in the backseat." I put the car in gear and headed across town in rush hour traffic to get Athyna to a hospital.

She coughed a few times while trying to talk. "So this is how sickness and pain feels?"

I looked at her in the rearview mirror, as she unfastened her weird-looking coat to examine her hurting side. I could make out an unusual style bruise. I turned around to get a better look and almost veered out of my lane.

"You're injured," I said. "You really do need to go to the hospital. Why didn't the police help you?"

"They didn't know," she said. She groaned a bit. Out of the mirror I could see her feeling around the sore area. She let out a strong yell and flicked a piece of metal towards the front, it hit the dash and bounced in my lap. I examined the small piece, which looked like the tip of a bullet.

"Are you shot?" I yelled. I turned around to see and increased acceleration at the same time – a terrible and dangerous driving combo.

"Don't worry about me," she said. "I don't have much time. We don't have much time."

"Stop talking," I said. "I'm going to get you to the hospital."

"The hospital can't help me," she said. From the rear-view mirror, I saw a small glow coming from her gunshot wound. I could also see a puff of dark smoke. It almost looked like a fire in the distant background, but I could swear this smoke trail was following us.

"What's going on with you," I asked as I turned around. I didn't see the smoke anymore. "That's funny, I thought I saw smoke."

"Erin, listen to me very carefully. Everything I told you last night was the truth. I need you to believe me." She coughed again and it seemed the light grew a little more intense. She turned around to see out of the back shield. "It's found me."

I looked again in the mirror and could see the smoke and Athyna's glow.

I yelled as I turned around to get a glimpse. "What's going on!" One thing for sure, something was different about this woman. "Just hold on, we'll be at the hospital soon."

"Erin, the smoke you see, if it reaches us it will kill me," she said as convincingly as possible. "I don't need a hospital," she said as she applied pressure to her side. I need a source of fresh water. I can get in touch with Jericho then."

"Why can I see it only in the mirror?"

"It's spiritual," she responded. "You won't see it in the flesh word, but because you're with me and you are starting to believe you may see it in other ways."

Athyna went on to talk about the angel who needed my help and as the glow became more and more concentrated, I started to believe more and more. As I turned corners the dark smoke followed, increasing its speed. I was doing almost 60 on the parkway and it was keeping pace. I started to panic.

I handed her a half full bottle of water from my drink holder. "Will this help," I yelled.

"Thanks, but I need to submerge myself in fresh, water" she said, with a united cough and laugh. The light grew even more, spreading past her wound to cover her chest area. Part of me wanted to get out of the car and leave, but I couldn't help but to believe.

My mind searched Baltimore for a fresh water source, but couldn't think of anything except the harbor, which we were more than 20 minutes away from, in addition, traffic would be gridlocked.

As I continued toward the East Side hospital, the city reservoir caught my eye. The reservoir, one of several, was Baltimore City's man made pond, which collected rain water to feed into the water system. Rain water had to be fresh, I thought.This one was located near the city's prized park. On a cold day like this, there shouldn't be too much attention given to us.

Athyna closed her eyes as the light grew bright like a baby sun. She moaned like she was in severe pain. The smoke travelled over cars behind us and was less than 10 feet away.

"Help me Lord to trust her," I whispered to myself, while pushing my car even faster.

"Hold on," I yelled. The smoke finally reached our car. Little by little it seeped through any cracks it could find. Athyna gagged loudly as I accelerated even more. "Almost there," I yelled. I drove over the grass and toward the reservoir. Apparently, a few police were sitting in their car watching our grass ride. The lights came on and sirens.

"You must keep going," she barely squeezed out. Her eyes began to roll back into her head. The light coming from her began to dim as more of the smoke entered into her body by mouth and nose.

I pressed on the accelerator even more as Athyna suggested and then all of a sudden my mind told me how unlike myself I was behaving. I'm driving 80 miles per hour over grass toward the resovoir with the police on my tail. I slammed on the brakes.

EVEN *Angels* NEED MIRACLES

Chapter 14

As Jericho made his way, the stares became so intense that for a moment, he decided he should go back. This wasn't the first time he journeyed down here. But this was the first time he'd journeyed without the authority from above.

With every footstep he took an increasing number of shadows arose and followed. They wanted to devour him badly. The screams of tormented souls echoed loudly as he approached the gate, which slowly swung open as if someone expected him.

"Jericho," whispered Ipos, the keeper of the gate. "You've taken an interest in the other side?"

"Don't be naïve," he answered as he walked in. "I need to speak to The Dark One."

"You've come without authority?" Ipos questioned. His slithery voice and hideous form almost convinced Jericho to put aside the idea of entering.

"What I've come with or without does not concern you."

"The moment you enter these gates, you are not protected. You could remain here forever," Ipos said with a sinister smile. "I tell you that not to warn or protect you, but to remind."

Jericho hesitated, and then slowly entered.

"Welcome." Ipos said. His smile was pure evil. Even with several missing teeth, his sinister grin was full. "Are you sure you want to do this?" The gates came to a loud close. "Nevermind."

Jericho looked to see the gate shut. He pushed slightly to check and indeed the gates were locked. He tried not to imagine being stuck in the shadow.

He walked past Ipos's station and made his way up the hill toward The Dark One's dwelling. Though Ipos would have loved to have his way with Jericho, he felt Iblis would appreciate handling Jericho himself.

The smell of sulfur and bile was putrid. Instant nausea made Jericho uneasy. Without authority, Jericho was made vulnerable to the stench, the fear, and whatever pain and torment he faced, should it be carried out. After a long moment's walk, he heard movement behind a larger stone.

"Jerichooooo," said the chant over and over from behind. A figure made his way into Jericho's sight. It was Olen – a fallen that Jericho had brought before the council ages ago. Olen decided to join with Geragan, who convinced him the ways of God were coming to an end. "Have you too lost your way," he moaned.

"I'm here for a reason and have not the time for talking with you."

"You banish me to this place and then you dare talk to me like that, without authority?"

Olen walked to Jericho with three other fallens that appeared out of the darkness. The hatred in their eyes burned with intensity.

Though somewhat intimidated, Jericho stood tall before the three. "Olen, I have no fight with you. And I did NOT send you here. You made a decision. You sent yourself here."

"Well you made a decision to come here today. And as I'm paying for my decision, you will certainly pay for yours. I only wish Geragan was here to enjoy this."

Olen snatched Jericho and threw him into the other fallens, who grabbed him lifting him off his feet. Jericho struggled to no avail. It was as though he had no strength. They took turns beating him and for the first time, he experienced pain as if any other soul or fallen." One fallen took a sharp bone from the ground and pierced Jericho's lower back. He screamed in torment.

After being thrown into a dead tree. He struggled to get up and grabbed an old thick root that resembled a strong cane. He swung it frightfully keeping Olen and the others away. Olen ordered the others to surround him using hand signals. In almost perfect timing, they all took small steps to eventually close in. Jericho and his stick had little effect on warding them away. When Olen finally grabbed Jericho again, a loud trumpet blared in the background. Olen and the others looked at each other in fear, seeming to forget all about Jericho. They took off and ran as the sound of footsteps came closer through the dense forest.

Jericho hid behind the large stone too tired and in pain to run.

A pack of demon possessed dogs and other beastly creatures made their way out of the forest and ran after Olen and the other fallens. One beast sniffed out Jericho from behind the stone and growled and hissed, causing Jericho to freeze in his place.

"Well done," said Malice, the demon leading the pack of wild beasts. "This may indeed earn a reward."

One of the demon creatures – a short, red horned beast - walked behind the stone to see what took so long for the pack to regroup.

"You go on," said Malice shooing the red horned beast away. "I'll take this prize to Iblis myself."

CHAPTER 15

After a brief nap, Aalon awoke feeling surprisingly well rested. He took some comfort in being able to actually sleep through some of his ordeal. The last thing he remembered was lying down and reading the Holy Scrolls. Before reading, Aalon tried over and over again to pray but felt a serious disconnection from the Lord. As he sat up from his half sitting – half lying position, he saw across from him a glass of water and what looked like a few rolls of fresh bread. Aalon pushed the bread aside, but sipped the water. Just as he sipped, he heard a knock and then the door inched its way open.

"Master Aalon?" said the whispering voice of what seemed to be a young female servant. "I've come to check on you."

"Do not call me master," Aalon said sternly. He wondered why she was sent. Looking at her, the woman seemed young and timid. Her healthy small frame and neatly combed bun suggested she had it better than most.

"Uh sorry mas–. I mean sorry, uhh… what would you prefer I call you." Her eyes lowered to suggest total submission.

"What do you want?" He asked – again without any compassion.

"I've come to fulfill any need you have. I trust your sleep was pleasant. I came in early to check on you and found you asleep. I took the scroll you were reading --"

Aalon frantically looked at the bed and saw the scroll was missing. "What did you do with it!" He said interrupting her.

"Nothing. I placed it back on the shelf." She walked over to show him, but was soon cut off from her action as he stood up to retrieve it himself."

"I'm sorry if I angered you," the young woman said sadly. "I shouldn't have touched it. I'm sorry. Please don't have me punished."

Aalon looked at her. "There's no punishment that would come from me." Aalon placed the scrolls near his pillow and sat back down. Hunger started to set in. He said a silent prayer and willed his hunger to cease.

"Thank you," she said. After a long weird silence she spoke again. "My name is Lorna. I am here to make sure you are comfortable. I brought you bread and water."

She saw that the bread was untouched. "Are you not hungry?" She asked.

"I'm fine," he said. "Your job is done."

"Uh- yes, well, okay I guess. Before I go, I am to let you know that there is a party to occur later and that you are invited to attend."

"I will not," he said.

"I just thought I would mention."

"Your job is done."

"Yes." Lorna picked up the tray with the bread and walked out. She gently closed the door behind her.

Iblis walked behind his wife and wrapped his arm around her waist. Delilah lifted his hand and pulled away.

"You dare reject me?" He asked in a harsh whisper, pulling her even tighter. He grabbed the back of her neck and spun her around to face him.

"Will you punish me more than what you are doing my love?" She asked.

"Believe me, when I say I will," he responded. His curiosity got the better of him however. Delilah, as beautiful as she was, still had the ability to weaken his defense just a little. "But tell me, how are you being punished?"

She paused. She knew she touched a nerve. "You have Aalon in a room as if he were a guest. I have heard you boast about his coming earlier and now that he's here, he gets treated as royalty. What does this mean?"

"You are right. I know that you've been patient with my plan. But I say this to you one time, this is bigger than that pawn. The only thing keeping me from having him screaming curses against his creator is the larger prize I seek. For now that is all you need to know."

In his signature clutch of her jaw line, he passionately kissed her.

"I'm sorry my master." Delilah said after the kiss ended.

"Don't be," he said. His firm grasp went from her jaw line to her throat. "I understand. But if you question me or prompt me to explain myself again. I will make sure that you really understand what real punishment is."

CHAPTER 16

As Iblis sat up from the bed. He walked to the mirror and saw the reflection of himself and his wife asleep in the bed behind him.

"Judgment day is almost here," he said as he grabbed the bottled beverage and poured himself a small glass. He raised it. "To me."

Knock Knock Knock.

He looked at the door as his wife sat up and pulled the sheets to hide her breasts.

"I'm not to be disturbed!" He shouted.

Knock Knock.

Iblis reached for his robe and walked to the door. His right hand throbbed for a life. He pulled the door forcefully and instantly reached out to snatch the throat of the one knocking.

"My master," Malice said as he gasped for air. "I'm sorry to have disturbed you. I have something you should see."

Iblis' grip became tighter as he lifted Malice off the floor even higher. Malice's eyes began to water from fear and pain.

"Mercy my master. I have something in your personal chamber, you'll be pleased."

Iblis released Malice as he fell to the floor.

"I'll be back," he said to his wife before closing the door.

"Malice, how long have you been a chaser?"

"I don't' remember," he said as they walked toward the chamber. Malice had been a chaser for almost as long as he had a memory. As a chaser, Malice would chase souls as a way to torment them. His subjects would flee for their lives forever. Occasionally, he would catch and torture them. Just when they felt their life would come to an end, the chains that bound them would rust away - and the chase would continue again. Those being chased would run beyond fatigue. Some would think that being a chaser was much better than being chased, but in actuality, neither was the better role to have. Occasionally, Iblis would check on Malice to see if he caught the assignments he gave to them. If he didn't he would be tortured by Iblis personally.

"Malice, if I find your interruption not as important as you say, all the torture I've given you and even the torture stored in me against God himself, will not equal the punishment I will place on your spiritual hide," he paused slightly before continuing. "And Malice."

"Yes, master?" He said while continuing his walk. The fear in his voice began to overtake the confidence he had when he ran across his prize.

"If you think your capture of Jericho was going to be a surprise to me and worth your release, guess what?"

Malice turned with a stuttering jaw. "H-h- how did you?"

"This is my hell remember. I'll deal with you later."

Malice immediately was carried away by shadows rising from the floor. His screams reached deafening levels, but not louder than the laughter coming from Iblis. He looked forward to making true of this threat to Malice. Out from behind the statue stepped the red horned beast, smiling at Iblis. He knew telling Iblis the good news before Malice would pay off and it did. The red horned beast received rest, while the screams of Malice continued. Surely, the fallens and the souls that he was assigned to chase were pleased at the sound, but not for long – as pleasure was never long lasting.

Iblis turned his attention to a bruised, bloodied Jericho who sat in the corner. He knew that Jericho crossed into his land, what he didn't know was why.

CHAPTER 17

Aalon grew restless. He wanted to know more about his situation. Although he could sleep, he felt the need to remain alert, after all he wasn't exactly at home. At least he hoped he wasn't.

It had been a long while since he ate and it was taking a toll. Two meals were brought before him since his refusal of the bread and each time he sent them back untouched. About the only thing he accepted was the water. He seemed to dehydrate easily, but his hunger bothered him more. He closed his eyes and began to pray again but was interrupted by the faint sound of laughter and music. It seemed to come from the halls outside his room.

The sounds were easy enough to ignore until his door swung open gently. Lorna appeared in the doorway. She was wearing what appeared to be formal wear. "My mast-, I mean Aalon. Today we are at festival. I would like to invite you to attend."

"You're wasting your time," he said as he laid back down unrolling what seemed to be a very lifeless scroll he held. "I am content in my quarters."

"Very well," she said sadly. She closed the door gently.

Aalon looked up. He was curious as to why she left so easily. It's not as if he wanted to go, but he felt a bit defenseless, not knowing what to expect.

He stared at the door while the faint laughter and music which became more highlighted to his senses appeared to grow just a bit louder. The festival which was taking place seemed just outside his door down the hall. He sat up, walked to the door and pressed his ear against it to listen.

The festival was definitely close. He reached for the latch on his door and gently opened the door. The moment he did, he saw Lorna standing in tears.

"Thank you," she said as she wiped her face.

Aalon frowned that his curiosity got the best of him. He began to close the door.

"No wait," she said. "Please, I'm begging."

Aalon closed the door and sat down. He sat down and began to pray but felt nothing. He didn't know why Lorna was crying, but he was touched.

He got up and gently opened the door. He stared at her as if to say, 'what do you want?'

"If I don't bring you to the festival, I'll be damned," she said.

He stared at her tear-soaked face. He handed her the napkin next to his untouched meal.

"You don't have to stay long," she softly spoke between her sobs. "I prayed for mercy and you opened the door."

Iblis lifted Jericho by his long beard to his feet. He could barely stand. He was worn and sore beyond belief. He appeared frightened of Iblis.

"So let me get this straight. You come here to try to get me to give you Aalon in exchange for you?"

Jericho just looked at him. Shortly after Iblis threw him into the wall. Jericho tightly closed his eyes as the impact almost crippled him. Though he knew his mission would not be easy, he was almost regretful of his decision to come.

"Look at you," Iblis said. "I bet you wish you'd stayed home today," he laughed.

Jericho laid there. He figured the more docile he behaved, the less aggression Iblis would respond with. It was time to initiate his plan. He forced a laugh through his pain. His blood-soaked teeth smiled at Iblis.

"You don't understand what you have here," Jericho said. The pain started to subside from his encounter with the wall. "Aalon is replaceable. There are plenty like him."

Jericho explained his willingness to trade places with him and reminded Iblis of his position as captain of the angel guard.

"Jericho my friend," Iblis said stooping down. He lifted Jericho's head with his finger to his chin. "You see, I have you both now. What makes you think I will let either of you leave?"

"You can only keep me as long as I am willing to stay. As captain I am able to come here and leave as I wish."

"But you came without the direction of your God. Therefore I am not obligated to allow you to leave. Jericho, you are mine."

Jericho stared at Iblis. The truth of the matter was that Iblis was right. He could keep him.

"But as much as I would love to keep you and cause you to curse your God, I'm going to turn down your offer. I'm going to send you back."

"Wha-what?" Jericho said. Why would you give up the-"

Iblis cut Jericho off and lifted him to his feet again. "This is my home! I'll do what I wish. Here, I'm sovereign!" He yelled.

"But – but. What do you want with him?"

"He is exactly what I need. And he is right where I want him."

"Iblis snatched Jericho to a curtain, which he opened to overlook the festival taking place in the courtyard. There, Aalon was seen walking among the party goers, holding the hand of a young woman as if he were having a good time.

"So, again while I would love to hurt you slowly, it would also serve me just as well to send you back to your home with confusion."

Iblis struck him one last time and then called servants to release Jericho.

"Yes my lord," the demon said as he placed Jericho on the back of a four legged beast as if he were a sack of cotton. Jericho's face looked more confused and frustrated than ever. Before the beast took off, Iblis approached him one last time.

"And Jericho, I don't say this much. In fact, I've never said this but it gives me great pleasure to say – "GET THE HELL OUT!"

CHAPTER 18

Kevin looked at his watch. It was nearing 11:00 a.m., and he was getting hungry. While he thumbed through Antonio's file, he wondered if he had made an impression on Erin. She was after all an excellent defense attorney, not only would his firm benefit from someone like that on his team, but it was obvious that the firm could benefit her in a few ways as well. He continued reading the file, but he could not stop thinking bout Erin. Since their days growing up, he held a passion for her.

First thing tomorrow, he would pay her another visit with breakfast. This time without any job-related pressure.

The patch of ice caused my car to spin out of control. The smoked-filled car nearly gagged me. I could tell things were bad. The car hit a steep curb and rolled down the hill uncontrollably, hitting the fence around the reservoir. My head hit the steering wheel on impact.

"Jericho!" Athyna yelled.

The car tumbled and landed in the reservoir. The ice cold water and thud from hitting my head were the last things I felt before seeing blackness surround me. Even the police sirens faded away.

CHAPTER 19

Aalon continued to make his way around the party. He wasn't there to have a good time. He merely promised to walk through for Lorna's sake. Oddly enough, it looked peaceful, though in an evil, demonic way, he thought. The attendees were dancing and carrying on to the strangest sound of live instruments. As he gazed around the room, he could see the center of attention was a tortured soul hung high, just above the band. A repetitive chant filled the room first beginning as a mumbling whisper and growing louder into a deafening roar, "flesh, flesh, flesh, flesh." He focused and stared at the hung soul. It was Sean, his human assignment. At the top of his lungs, Aalon screamed and leaped into the air. Though it took nearly all his strength, he managed to fly towards Sean and loosen his straps. He floated back down to the floor and held the lifeless soul close as demons did their best to tear him away.

"Get back," Aalon ordered to the deaf ears. They soon overpowered him and took Sean out of the room. Aalon was powerless to protect him. All he could do was scream.

There were many stares as he sat down in total tiredness. This was the same feeling he had when he tried to revive him. Demons walked by, obviously ordered to not lay a hand on him. If pleasure was at all possible, each demon, evil spirit and beast took pleasure in watching Aalon weep.

"I didn't know," Lorna said. "You must believe me," she knelt beside him and held him near.

Iblis drew the drapes closed as if watching a powerful scene come to an end. Out of all the evil beings taking pleasure in Aalon's and Sean's misfortune, Iblis was pleased the most.

Aalon wiped his tears and whispered to Lorna. "You've gotten me to come, now I'm going back." She just stared. She had nothing to say. She felt hurt leading him to that site and sort of wished he refused to attend, though the payment for her failure would have been stern. "Good bye," he said. He turned around to walk away.

As unwise as it was, Lorna decided to join him.

"Wait, I'm coming with you," Lorna followed as he walked out of the area.

"Go back to your party," he said. He didn't even turn to look at her.

"Wait, Aalon." Aalon paused and turned.

"You may not have saved him," she said. She grabbed his arm. "But you saved me."

He just looked at her. He wanted to speak freely but cut himself short of opening his mouth. He wondered if all this was a set up for more hurt.

They made their way back to his quarters. Aalon slowly paced the room. His mind turned and his thinking began to get more clear. Perhaps there was something he could do to help himself, he thought.

"Can I get you something?" She asked. She felt worried in part because of Aalon's defiance, she also couldn't stop thinking what Iblis would do if he discovered Lorna's growing concern for Aalon

"No," he said, as he ignored the growling of his hunger.

"You can't possibly be okay. You've eaten nothing since you've arrived. Let me prepare you a tray of--"

"No. I'm not ready to eat," he said.

"I see, well, do you feel like talking," she said.

"Oh, we have much to talk about. Lock the door."

CHAPTER 20

"Jericho, do not move," said an elder angel as he touched Jericho's bruised and burned figure. Jericho shook in pain. His scars and wounds from his recent beating were rapidly healed away. He sat up panting and looked around at the others, who must have found him after he'd been cast out of hell – the first time for any being.

Questions from each overwhelmed him.

"Why did you go?"

"What possessed you to interfere?"

"You are fortunate that you were cast out."

"Please tell me my Erin did not die!"

Jericho sat up at Ella's voice, while the entire group of angels also turned to see who this frenzied voice belong to.

"Ella," Jericho said as he stood to his feet still weakened from his experience, but quickly regaining his strength. "She's here? Then Athyna did it. This is great. Trust me."

The others listened as he spoke. They were all confused by his rambling. "What's this about?" asked one angel.

"Who is this?" asked another pointing to Ella.

"Please," he said as he turned to the group. "I must talk with Ella alone. I thank you for your care. I am well now. Believe me I am well."

They stood in silence, but one by one they left allowing them their private moment.

"They will not allow me to see her. What happened?" she asked." "Where is Athyna?"

"Come, we'll go together. It will be okay."

"I had no idea what would happen at the party," Lorna said softly as Aalon poured himself a drink of water. She took the pitcher from his hand and continued with his pouring before handing him his drink. "It's important to me that you know that." He stared at her. He knew that he was getting weak. He forced himself not to show it. He looked longingly at the water she held in her hand.

"It's okay," she said. "You can have the water. It cannot be damned." By that, she meant it wouldn't build toward a fleshly state. Food on the other hand, even fruit, would stir up carnal thinking and desires in no time.

He still stared and then slowly brought the water to his mouth.

"I know that you are hungry Aalon," she said as he sat on his bed.

"If I eat, I'll develop a fleshly nature."

"But if you do not eat, you will also weaken."

"Are you enjoying my battle," he asked.

"Aalon, I wish to see no one fall," she said. "I will not bring harm to you."

Aalon stood up in anger. He hated his situation and wished this entire ordeal would make more sense to him. Had he received the torture he expected, his will and discipline would strengthen his spirit. But this freedom presented all kinds of danger. He would have to guard himself continually and act as cunning as his enemies.

"Tell me about you," he said.

"About me?"

"Yes, you," he said. "You are to serve me? Why? Why are you so - so privileged with comfort?"

She turned away. Never had she considered her role as comfortable. Every time she got close to someone it was for one purpose, to weaken them for torture. She either succeeded in her task, or faced their punishment. And if Iblis thought she was taking too long, she received torture still. Little did Aalon realize it, but she hated her situation as much, as he hated his, if not, more.

Hell presented all sorts of punishment in addition to the pain of burning. Some punishments only disguised themselves as having a few more advantages to those not suffering that fate, but all forms were tailor made methods of cruelty. None were comfortable. The constant feeling of being chased. Everlasting stillness, where torture awaited anyone who showed even the tiniest movement. The list went on and brought painful images to Lorna's mind as she thought about them.

"You are a fallen?" He asked.

"No, I am a soul."

In hell, fallens and souls were often difficult to tell apart. In heaven, there was a clear distinction between angels and souls.

"I'm sorry," he said.

"I am too." She walked to the water and ran her finger slowly around the rim of the glass. "I've been here a long time. I would say hundreds of human years. But I don't know how long, no one does. You think you have a sense of time only to discover there's no such thing. I don't even remember my time on earth. I would wager that you do not even know how long you have been here. Aalon paused to think about it.

"That tormented soul – from the party, you knew him didn't you?"

Aalon clinched his hands together showing his stress and slowly shook his head. "He was mine to protect and I failed him."

"Failed him?"

"He's here because of me."

"That's not possible," she corrected. "Everyone here is here because of their own choice – even Iblis." Lorna turned to Aalon and found a look of anger that frightened her.

"He should have had more time," he demanded.

"We all are given enough time." She couldn't believe how much her own position has changed. She remembered feeling like Aalon a long time ago.

"Where is he?" Aalon walked to Lorna and stared deeply into her eyes. It was the first time he showed any sign of needing her.

"Where is who?"

"Sean. The tortured soul from the party"

"I don't know, he could be anywhere. He's not under your watch anymore."

"I need to find him," Aalon said.

Just then the door swung open wildly. "Find who?" There standing in the doorway was Iblis. And he looked displeased with everything.

CHAPTER 21

Lorna's head immediately dropped. Though, she knew it wasn't allowed, she prayed there would be no torture for either.

"Leave us," he said.

She left without question. Before she made it out, Iblis forcefully grabbed her arm. He placed his face directly in front of hers.

"If this task is too much for you, I can find you another purpose."

"No my Lord," she said.

He released her and let her walk out. The door closed gently.

"How have you found my little… " He looked around the room and smiled. "Hell?"

Aalon didn't answer.

"Don't speak," he said. "In due time we'll talk. Jericho was just here and wanted to exchange himself for you." He waited to study Aalon's reaction, who purposely tried not to show any. "You should feel honored. A captain for a guardian? Not to worry though. I told our good friend from the other side you were in good hands," he said.

Aalon stared into Iblis' eyes as if he were trying to read deeper into Iblis than his words. As a guardian, he's had plenty of experience in people reading. He couldn't get anything from Iblis though. But instinctively he knew nothing good existed in him.

"What's on your mind?" Iblis questioned. He felt Aalon's penetrating stare.

Aalon just looked at him.

"Why I didn't take Jericho for you?" He walked to the bread and dipped it into the sauce before he popped it in his mouth. He closed his eyes to savor the taste. "How about what this is all about?" In a flash, Iblis had moved in front of Aalon almost nose to nose, his eerie smile was just about ear to ear. "Maybe you'd like to know what I'm going to do with you?"

"I do have a question," Aalon said.

Iblis' smile drew narrower. "Ask." He said scowling.

"Are you always this frightened?"

Iblis' eyes widened, his rage at maximum boil. He lifted Aalon by his throat while staring hard into his eyes.

"You dare ask me if I'm afraid? I fear nothing!" He threw Aalon into the corner which caused him to almost turn over the furniture in his quarters. Aalon, shaken up, but not hurt, stayed down and just stared.

"It is you who should be in fear," Iblis snarled. "For the order, which you're used to is ending soon. And while I may not be able to put my hands on you – yet I can certainly have my way with Sean. Trust me when I say he will pay dearly!

He turned and walked out. The door slammed closed behind him causing the tray of bread to drop to the floor.

Aalon stayed in the corner. He tried to fight back another round of crying as he thought of what Sean may go through. He had to do something.

Suddenly a quiet knock and the door slowly opened. Lorna peeked in.

"Are you alright?" She asked as she hurried to him and tried to help lift him up. He managed to get up without her assistance.

"I'm okay." He said He wiped his eyes dry with the palm of his hands. "Tell me, is there a library here."

"Yes, but."

"But what?"

"I'm forbidden to even discuss it."

"Why would you take such an unwise risk?" Athyna hugged Jericho after he entered the room. She heard about his visit with Iblis. "You might have never returned."

"Perhaps there's a lot of unwise decisions going around," he answered.

They hugged a while longer before Athyna broke away to look at him.

"How's Aalon? Did you see him?"

Iblis showed him to me."

Athyna gasped, covering her mouth. The thought of Aalon's torment struck her mind with horrid images.

"It is okay, he is not harmed." He said. "It looks as though Iblis is trying to tempt him."

"Where is Erin? How is she?" Jericho asked changing the subject. "Her grandmother is worried."

"She's okay," Athyna said. She's resting. We can take her grandmother in soon."

"How did you get her to believe," he asked.

"My dire situation convinced her. Perhaps it was ordained after all," Athyna said. All of a sudden it hit her that Jericho was allowed to return. "Why did Iblis allow you to leave?"

"I still don't know. I wanted to switch Aalon's place for mine. Since I had no authority to be there, and he knew it, he could have kept me and Aalon. But he sent me back. It makes no sense."

"This troubles me deeply." Athyna said. "He could have kept a captain, but decided not to? There must be something we don't see."

"We will figure it out. Hopefully not too late."

CHAPTER 22

I felt a gentle rocking as I slowly opened my eyes from what seemed like a peaceful nap. My eyes tried hard to focus. The light from the room grew more intense by the second. I couldn't bring anything into focus. Slowly, sight and sound became more clear until I could make out Athyna leaning above me. Almost instantly, the memory of the car crash flashed before me and I sat up quickly, too weak to scream, I started to pant.

"Easy," she said as she kept me from jumping out of bed. "Everything is going to be fine Erin. It will all make sense in a moment. You must pace yourself. Give yourself time to adjust."

"What do you want from me," I asked. I looked around the unfamiliar room as my senses started to react. Strangely I became more curious than fearful. It was almost as if I couldn't find fear in me. "Where are we?"

"We're home. Actually, you're in my home." Athyna said.

I finally managed to sit up to get a look. From the looks of things, this looked like a very nice setting. Very clean and organized. Everything matched. Lots of books, plants writings on scrolls and sunlight. It was peaceful and comfortable.

"Jericho will join us soon. He needed to take care of some urgent matters."

A quick memory flash hit me again, where I saw Athyna reach over the back seat to protect me seconds before the impact. Finally my full memory returned.

"The accident! Are we okay?" I tried to get up, but my strength was not there. It was as if I were in dream state. My body felt like it just didn't want to respond.

"Yes dear, we are fine. You saved my life," Athyna said. She sat at my bedside holding my hand. "Rest a little more. When Jericho arrives, we'll explain it all."

"What's going on with me? Explain what?" As much as I wanted to sit up and get all the information I could, as much as I wanted to ask questions to gain understanding, I couldn't resist the weary feeling over me; almost as if I were drugged. I wanted nothing more than to continue resting, I closed my eyes and went back to sleep.

CHAPTER 23

"She's stable. Her vitals show no signs of serious damage. The coma however is something that we just don't know anything about. I do know that she is showing normal brain activity. That's a very good sign."

"Thank you Dr. Patterson," Audrey said as she held onto Erin's hand. She used the other hand to wipe her tears. "Erin, you're going to be all right. I'm right here."

"Kevin is this going to be a problem for you," David asked. He obviously didn't share the same concern about possibly being disbarred. As he laid on the massage table turning up his blue tooth in his ear, trying not to clue Kevin in on his tropical vacationing, he shooed the masseuse away to speak to Kevin a bit longer.

"Sir, Antonio is falsifying his whereabouts," Kevin said. "If he lies under oath and I willingly represent him knowing so, it could look bad not only for me but the firm."

"Who's going to tell," he asked. "I'm not. Listen Kevin, Mr. Walker is paying good money for the best representation. You're one of our best. You're in line to make partner in less than a year. Please tell me you can handle this."

Kevin thought about his partnership. He's played fair and square since his first trial and was proud of that fact. He knew he was clever enough to figure how to make this work. "I can handle it." He responded.

"Good to hear." David said. "Let's talk about strategy in a few days."

"You got it."

They both hung up. Kevin leaned back in his chair clasped his hands behind his head and thought about making partner. He also thought about possible alternatives to letting Antonio lie under oath. He stared at his integrity award he received last year from the the daily newspaper until he was interrupted by the ringing of his personal cell phone. He could see it was Erin. Probably decided to come on board, he thought.

CHAPTER 24

"Hey baby, wake up," said the sweet voice in my ear. I opened my eyes and saw a beautiful woman sitting at my bed side. It took a moment for my sight to adjust, but not nearly the amount of time it took earlier.

"Grandma?" I asked. She rubbed my forehead and gently brushed back the front of my hair as always. She looked about 50 years younger from the last time I saw her.

She laughed, "Wow, no one calls me that here, but yes, it's me. Are you okay?" she asked.

I finally was able to sit up, although slowly. I could see Athyna and Jericho in the back of the room watching us. They both started to make their way over.

"Grandma, where am I? Am I –" I hesitated to think I had been killed in the car accident.

"No, you're not dead. But you're not home right now either. I think this is the part that, well, I'll let Athyna and Jericho talk to you because I don't fully understand it myself."

All of a sudden what seemed like a surge of soft energy came upon me. The first thing I noticed was the smell of the room. It resembled expensive candles. A constant, pleasant aroma. Also, I could see and hear with such clarity. All my senses seemed heightened – including the sense of touch as my grandmother's hand continued to brush my hair from my face, giving me an almost tingling sensation.

My grandmother stood up from the bed and motioned for Athyna and Jericho to come forward.

"Grandma, don't leave."

"Baby, I'm not going anywhere. We'll talk, but as I understand it, you're desperately needed. I'll talk to you again. I promise." She hugged me one more time and gave me a kiss on my cheek. Then she hugged Athyna and Jericho before they approached my bedside. By that time, I managed to sit up fully with my legs hanging over the side of the bed.

I tried to stand and instantly fell to the ground. Athyna rushed to my side to help me up.

"What was that about?" I asked. "I feel like this is the first time I've ever walked."

"Well, technically, it is," Athyna said as she helped me sit back down. "At least this is the first time you've walked without your earthly body."

My earthly body? I looked at my hands and arms which appeared to be normal. Frantically, I looked for a mirror. None existed.

"Even if we had mirrors, you wouldn't see a difference," Athyna said. "You look the same as you did on earth, trust me. But you should feel the difference."

I felt my face and slowly edged my way back to the floor. "So this is heaven? This is where everyone on earth is striving to make it," I said as I put my full weight on the floor and surprisingly found my sense of balance. I held onto the bed for support and tried to take a baby step. "I don't believe it."

"What's there not to believe?" Jericho responded. "Look around you. You are here with us as Athyna said you'd be."

"This is not the heaven I expected." I said

"You are in heaven," Jericho said. "But because you are not completely in the spiritual state, you're limited to what your natural mind can see. That's to be expected and no getting around that. As your sprit grows in strength, so shall your ability to see. Tell me, am I and Athyna wearing wings and halos?"

I looked around and then stared at Athyna, although she looked better groomed, she didn't look too different from when I saw her on Earth.

"As Jericho said, you'll be able to see even more clearly and your senses will really improve. Even your thinking will start to change," Athyna said.

For some strange reason, I just started crying. It wasn't that I was sad or upset, or frightened. It just happened. Athyna hugged me tight. "It's okay Erin. We will all be okay." I cried even more. "You just need some time. Jericho, can you give us a moment?"

Even with this new world around me, I felt as though I still needed assurance that I wasn't losing my mind. I needed convincing that all this was real. All this hope they placed in me was intimidating.

"This is all happening too fast," I said wiping my eyes. "Why me?"

"Because you're the perfect person for the job, Athyna said You're excellent in the courtroom. You know that. You're smart and honest."

"Aren't there plenty of angels you can go to? What about those attorneys that are no longer on earth?

"Those who are still awaiting judgement day cannot serve in the courts. And well, an angel representing Aalon would only feed into Iblis' bias claim. Erin, you are unpredictable. All humans are. Iblis will be off guard."

"What do you mean?"

"I mean, you have free will. You can be as crafty as he, without going against the purpose for good. Angels were created to be truthful – always. You ask us a question, we tell you the answer. We ask questions to seek understanding not to strategically get answers."

I just listened to Athyna as she went on about how qualified I was. The more she spoke, the more confident I became. My tears started to dry away and I felt more at ease. I can't say I was over my nervousness, but I was at the point of accepting my belief.

"Some help I'm turning out to be," I said between sniffles and laughter.

"It's okay. We'll help each other." Athyna said.

Jericho turned to leave with my grandmother.

For what seemed like the equivalent of a full day, Jericho and Athyna answered questions and helped me figure out how to do everything I needed. From walking to getting dressed, it was really like I was a child all over again, but given how much I had to learn, it really didn't take long for me to adjust. Athyna kept reminding me that I would learn much quicker in heaven than on Earth since I'm able to focus without distraction. After Jericho and Athyna left, I dressed myself in a one piece suit. My hair was pulled in a tight bun. Everything seemed normal. According to Jericho, this outfitt could be completely different from what others in heaven see as my mind can only see earth-style clothes. I stared at things to see if they'd change before my eyes. Nothing happened. I was a bit disappointed to be quite honest. I wanted to see clouds. I wanted to fly. I wanted to see all the things I always believed heaven to be as a child.

When Athyna and Jericho returned, I figured I'd ask a few more questions about what's happened to me and my body on Earth. "How's Audrey?"

She was all the family I had.

"You're in a peaceful sleep state. A coma. You're fine. Everything is moving along as normal. Your loved ones are praying for your return. Or should I say awakening. You'll come out of this."

In a strange way, I had the feeling that I was the target of a cruel and elaborate joke. The other feeling I had was that I was deceiving my friends back home. I mean, here I was comfortable and they were, I'm sure, experiencing sadness or at least, I kind of hoped they were.

"I'm sure it's out of the question to send them a message," I started.

"It's best not to," Athyna said. She paused, looked out of the window and turned back to me. "Let us go out." Athyna said.

"Go out? I said surprised. Though heaven should have had me anxious to wander, the desire to run around and explore didn't enter my mind as much as what was going on back home.

"Yes," Athyna answered. "Let us go out. I want to show you as much as you can take.

EVEN *Angels* NEED MIRACLES

CHAPTER 25

As Lorna and Aalon walked through the halls, they walked past torture rooms and fear chambers where souls and fallens pleaded for mercy. Along the way, they walked past demons that salivated for the opportunity to devour them both. They kept walking and found their way through a dark corridor that led to Iblis' reading room.

"If he knew I led you here, we both would pay dearly," she pleaded. "We can still go back."

"If you must go back, I understand," Aalon said. He stared at her as she eventually unlocked the door and opened it. Inside were books and bound volumes of writings that was second only to the library he frequented in heaven. He walked around taking in the abundance of Iblis' collection. He gently pulled the spines of a few books to get a better look -- writings on persuasion, poetry about fear, and even collections about faith and struggle lined half the wall. There were also drawers and cabinet spaces that were too multitudinous to fully explore. After much walking Aalon finally found a locked door without a knob or any other sort of means for opening it. "This is Iblis' private study," Lorna said. "No one has ever entered in this room – not even his wife. It is rumored that even God himself has no knowledge of its contents."

Aalon pushed on the door with all his might, but it wouldn't give. It wouldn't even make a creaking noise as if it recognized it was being pushed. Just then, he heard footsteps coming from behind the door. There was no place to hide. Before the door opened, Lorna gripped Aalon's shoulder and they bot disappeared into the floor.

Iblis stepped out. He felt the presence of an intruder, actually two intruders. He wasn't completely sure, but he trusted his instincts. He looked around and saw no signs of anyone. Perhaps he was simply feeling anxious about the plan he was unfolding. The plan that would, without exaggeration, ruin time, existence and faith. He was definitely excited, but he knew better than to simply dismiss his gut feeling about the intrusion. He walked to survey the room closely and noticed a book of poetry slightly out of place. He grit his teeth and disappeared in a cloud of smoke.

A minute after Iblis vanished, Lorna and Aalon finally materialized. Aalon fell to his knees, clutching his gagging throat. His nostrils worked to breathe but were useless. Lorna leaned him back and kissed him, drawing out smoke, sulfur gases and other vile elements. It took quite a bit for him to regain his breathing.

"What happened?" He questioned barely able to talk.

"I took you to the lake of fire. It's the darkest part of his kingdom. It was the only way to keep us from his sight. "We must go back to your quarters, I'm sure he is attuned to our meddling.

"I'm not afraid of him," Aalon said barely able to breathe. He looked up and saw the door left open, and made his way inside. On the table a few steps from the door, lay a scroll. Aalon picked it up and unwound its contents. He studied the writings and was shocked at what he came across. He looked around the room and saw books, many of which focused on the same theme. Suddenly it made sense at what his role was in this whole event. He'd hold onto this new knowledge until it was time for him to play his hand.

"Interesting," Aalon exclaimed. "Lorna, we can leave now," he said as he turned around.

She was nowhere to be found.

CHAPTER 26

We left the room and made our way to a very lush park. The smell and colors from the wild floral arrangement created an ensemble of visual perfection. No litter, no graffiti, nothing existed that served as pollution or a spoiler for the scenery. Everything was in its proper place. The gentle breeze of the freshest air and the entire environment engulfed me. I was mesmerized by my surroundings. Colors that I've never seen and couldn't describe suddenly appeared.

"There's no dust," Athyna said.

"Huh?"

"No dust in the air. No tiny particles of human flesh."

I twisted my face in disgust.

As I sat down on the bench to enjoy the experience, I started to notice all the stares coming from so many.

"They'll get over it," Athyna said. "They've been instructed to not bother you."

"They wouldn't bother me," I said.

"Trust me. Yes they would," Athyna said. It's not like they get to see a temporary visitor every day."

"There's never been a visitor here?"

"You're the first."

Not only did colors start to become more vivid, but new colors began to form all together. Even new shapes and architecture caught my eye. There were buildings that definitely could have passed for earth structures as well as buildings that were so unique in design; they defied the laws of physics. Even building material superseded anything I've seen before. Buildings didn't stay within the concrete grey color family. Jade, taupe, rose, colors that were reserved or limited to natural or playful structures could be found everywhere. We walked toward a magnificent columned structure that had a massive gate around it. This is the courthouse," Athyna said.

"This looks like a typical court house structure," I mentioned. I hoped she didn't notice my frown but I was a bit disappointed again that there wasn't much difference.

When we walked in I saw a collection of scrolls, books and writings that no library on earth could match. Shelves of writings expanded an almost infinite height and width. After following Athyna down a couple of corridors, we finally reached a table with one heavy book resting in the center.

"This is everything you need to know about Aalon."

"Who?"

"Aalon, the angel you will be representing."

"Oh." I said suprisingly, "everything about Aalon is contained in this?"

"Exactly."

Before I opened the book, Athyna gave me all the background she could recall.

Athyna described Aalon as being very good hearted. As a guardian angel, Aalon was considered one of the most talented guardians on hand; he had a knack for casting out demons, which he learned from Jericho. They stood no chance when he was on duty. Aalon always provided the best guardianship he could muster. He understood early on that among a myriad of tasks and responsibility, his core assignment was to watch over and protect his assignment. He kept a regular log, chronicling the life of his humans and his involvement in certain situations. He provided companionship whenever possible. The book looked as though it contained tens of thousands of pages.

"I'll need something to write on and write with," I asked.

"You won't need to take any notes," she replied and nudged the book closer to me.

Athyna went on to tell me more about Aalon and his assignment Sean, while I flipped open the book and read more about his background and the various assignments he's protected. In heaven, not only was I able to read pages quickly, but my comprehension was crisp. It was as if I was speed reading, except I could recall everything I read word for word. I was surprised at my enhanced ability. I pushed myself to read faster and I did. I was getting in about 40 -50 pages per minute. It seemed as if I coldn't max out. It was amazing. When I came across information concerning his most recent assignment, Sean Logan–a problem child that Aalon was faced with having to guard with extreme care, I became fixated. Athyna left me to my studying for a while as I engrossed myself in the mischievous ways of Sean. Drug use, drug pushing, gambling, gang life, prison–his rap sheet was extremely long. I dog- eared the page and closed the book to rest my eyes. It wasn't that they were literally tired, but I wanted to see what else was here.

CHAPTER 27

Iblis opened the door to an empty room. No sign of Aalon or Lorna. "I see they chose to make this interesting," Iblis whispered to himself. He turned to see that the bread was still on the floor. He felt Lorna might develop care for him all along. She knew the price to pay for such treachery. It was a while since the last time she paid for a mistake. She was obviously overdue. He would take great pleasure in reminding her of the cost.

"Forgive me for interrupting you master, but they found a representative for Aalon. She wishes to speak to him." Geragan stepped back after presenting the news and prepared to walk away. With such a long history together, he knew Iblis could appreciate news and at the same time strike for being disrupted from thought.

"She?" He questioned. "Who is this she?"

"A human master."

"Do not game with me," Iblis said in a most serious tone. "They wouldn't dare!"

"My Lord, I made certain of this before I came to you."

"Her name?"

"Erin is all I know master."

"She could be any of the millions of Erin's I know," Iblis rubbed his chin as if an idea was beginning to form. "Well, Geragan as you can see, Aalon's not here, but I will pay a little visit to the Holy Kingdom. While I'm out, find the angel and Lorna."

Iblis walked out slowly.

Geragan silently let out a sigh and rested against the wall. He just never knew what Iblis' reaction would be.

CHAPTER 28

After walking around and observing, I sat back down to dive into the book. I was almost half way finished. More and more pages seemed to fly by. I was beginning to get a strong picture of Aalon for myself. I looked forward to meeting him. Athyna was arranging the visit as I studied and prepared for the hearing. Just as I was starting to really appreciate the silence, I felt a strange presence and heard a very soft, yet disturbing laughter.

"You're it? You are the angel's messiah," questioned the laughing character as he placed himself in the empty chair next to me. "Forgive me, forgive me for laughing."

I just stared. Something about his presence told me he wasn't a friend.

"You must tell me your name," he said. "Your whole name."

Before I could say anything, he closed his eyes and said my whole name with a smile.

"Erin Crawford. Let's see, Baltimore, Maryland. You're 35 or 36, I can't quite remember. You've got a lot of anger in you. Possibly from being an orphan, possibly for all the suppression and resistance you give yourself rather than taking advantage of some of the things you'd prefer in life. You've got a pretty good hedge around you though. I haven't been able to break open that wall – yet."

I stared in shock. I was speechless and confused.

"Oh forgive me for not introducing myself," he said. "I'm The Dark One. You know Satan, the devil, Lucifer, and all the other names I've lived up to."

I stood up ready to make a break for it, when he quickly placed his hands on my shoulders and forced me to sit down. "Do not get up on my account."

I couldn't move. And as much as I tried to scream, I couldn't. He was incredibly strong and my intimidation wasn't helping much.

"Take your hands off her. You are not welcome here," Athyna quickly walked toward us. Iblis saw her dashing toward us and turned to face her for confrontation. To anger her further, he grabbed a fist full of my hair and jerked me backwards. Though there was no pain, I fell over off balance.

Athyna grabbed his hand and made him release my hair only for him to turn the hold onto her wrist and bring her to her knees. Apparently, his strength was a concern for her as well.

"I'm always welcome here," he said. "I was welcomed here when you were still a breeze in your master's nostrils."

"Let her go," I said. I knew I couldn't offer much help, but I refused to sit there and allow him to attack her.

They both turned toward me as I stood up.

"Erin don't," Athyna said. He pushed her to the floor and walked toward me while two shadows from the floor rose up to hold her down.

"You've got a fire in you," he said as he moved toward me almost nose to nose. "Good, you'll need that."

He grabbed my throat and instantly snatched my breath from me.

"You are not fully protected mind you," he said as he lifted me off the ground. "I could end this here!" Athyna struggled to get free, but she was overpowered.

I didn't know whether fear or the fact that he was incredibly strong paralyzed me more.

"Iblis be gone!" Jericho shouted as he stormed through the door. He drew a sword from his side. "Or it will most certainly be ended here."

He let go of my throat and walked toward Jericho. Jericho held the tensed sword's position at a perfect angle aimed at his head. Iblis froze in motion and stared back at Jericho.

"Seems you healed quite nicely," he said to Jericho. He turned to me, "This will be too easy. I welcome seeing you again."

CHAPTER 29

"I need to get a postponement for the arraignment hearing," Kevin said while staring over Erin's lifeless, tube connected body. The rhythmic pulse of the breathing machine made it hard for him to focus. It was obvious that the person on the other end of the phone was giving him a hard time with rescheduling. "We'll talk about this tomorrow," he said. He hung up the hospital room phone. Audrey scrolled through her cell phone and called number after number to cancel appointments as well. She also checked Erin's phone for numbers and appointments.

The nurse walked in and pointed at Audrey sternly.

"You'll have to use that outside in the lobby," she said as she walked toward Erin's monitors to check vitals.

Kevin turned off his blackberry and slid it back into the holster as Audrey folded her cell phone shut.

"How is she?" Audrey asked.

"We're still not sure. While she is unconscious, she doesn't carry any of the other signs connected with a coma," she said. She fiddled with a few of the buttons on the monitors, jotted down a few notes and changed her IV solution. It's kind of strange, but honestly it seems like she's just sleeping. Did any of you see what happened?"

"No," Audrey answered. "I just received a phone call from the police who arrived on the scene." Audrey started to cry as Kevin instinctively provided a hug to comfort her. The doctor came in to receive the chart from the nurse as she walked out.

"Hi, I'm Dr. Conaway," he said.

"So you think she's going to come out of this?" Kevin asked the doctor.

"Only time will tell," he responded. He flipped through the chart and adjusted one of the monitors to the right. "Her vitals look good. It honestly appears that she could wake at any time. We just need to be patient and have faith.

Aalon made it back to his room without any trouble. He was relieved that he could finally lie down. The stress from sneaking through the corridors, hearing the screams of tormented souls and imagining any one of them as coming from Sean was a big weight for him to carry. Angels have lost assignments to the dark side before, and each time the guardian angel felt a sense of failure and loss. Actually seeing the human you're watching in hell puts an even greater burden on the angel's shoulder as Aalon learned. He dropped onto his bed wearily. It didn't take long before he started to drift to sleep. The appreciated peace however was violently interrupted as his room door flew off the hinges and two large fallens walked in and snatched Aalon to his feet.

"You've been summoned," said one of them.

They each took him by an arm.

As he walked down the hall way, he noticed two other fallens and a few demons escorting Lorna away. She slowed down and looked at him in apologetic fashion. The demon directly behind her jabbed her in the back with his walking stick.

"Keep moving!" he said. "He's the reason why you're going to the chamber in the first place."

"Where are they taking her?" Aalon questioned the two fallens rushing him down the corridor.

"It's none of your concern," said the larger fallen. "Be glad it's not you."

CHAPTER 30

Kevin woke up suddenly. He hadn't found a comfortable position in his chair all night. The several 15 - 20 minute cat naps he squeezed in didn't do anything to satisfy his tired body. Just when he started to drift, a nurse walked in to monitor Erin's vitals, or he would hear loud beeping coming from the machine. He looked around the room. The clock on the wall showed nearly 7:00 a.m. On the other side of the room, he saw Audrey snoring in the recliner. What he would give for just 10 minutes on that rickety old thing, he thought to himself. He decided to get some coffee to stay awake, since he couldn't get any sleep. Kevin made his way down the hall, passing doctors, nurses and sleeping loved ones of patients stretched out over lobby chairs. He was deeply concerned for Erin. For years, he's carried a secret love for her, deeper than any of the superficial relationships he's had throughout his dating experience. Erin was supposed to be his one. He honestly felt that. It literally frightened him – the idea that he may never get that perfect time to share his feelings. He prayed during his brief elevator ride and was soon in the cafeteria, paying for a small coffee and a newspaper. The room was jarringly quiet as he made his way to a table.

Geragan stood in the locked bathroom and stared at himself in the mirror as he shifted into the form of a doctor. He was a handsome man, wearing a very convincing doctor look – complete with lab coat and stethoscope. "Hi, I'm Doctor Dan," he said in a slight chuckle. Geragan understood his mission, and was not about to fail. Iblis wanted insurance. It wasn't that he lacked confidence in his ability to beat a human in court, but he needed to ensure that Erin didn't' win. Just Kevin's signature, Geragan thought to himself. Then Iblis would have the insurance he needed. Most people thought trading their soul away was fairytale or in the movies. People have sold their soul since creation. Among all the other fallens or demons that existed, Geragan was probably the most polished at this task. To him, it gave an opportunity to practice his acting. He was a fan of theater and when possible, he would attend plays and movies on earth. He was responsible for a several actors, who gave up their soul for riches and fame. None of them got to see old age. Some died only a year or two right after their fame kicked in. He smiled at the thought of those suckers. Now, should I be the doctor who needs his signature in order to save Erin's life? He wondered to himself. Probably too much of a legal issue. "Remember Geragan, he's a lawyer" he said to himself. He shifted into a very attractive woman, "Perhaps a cutie who could get him to treat her to breakfast and pay for the meal with his credit card." He ruled that out. He probably would not fall for that given the state of his love interest. "Ah ha! He said, I'll go as little old Mattie." He pretty much patted himself on the back for the decision. Mattie hadn't been used in years. A very passive-aggressive, gentle middle aged woman, who reminds everyone of their mom or grandmother. He made sure to have all his essentials, from cute outfit to large handbag. Before heading out, he signed his clipboard with 30 – 40 fake names and then dropped it into the large bag. "It's show time," he said to himself.

Just as Kevin took his first sip and folded his paper to an article he was interested in reading, an older woman approached him in a kind gentle voice.

"Excuse me young man," she said. He looked up and smiled. "Will you be here a while? You look like such a nice man. Would you mind watching my bag, I just want to go get me some breakfast.

"I'll be hear a while longer, sure I'll watch your bag."

"I'm Mattie by the way, and you are?"

"Kevin," he said.

"Thanks Kevin."

She walked to the food station. "Can I get you anything?"

"I'm good, but thank you."

It has been a while since Mattie had Earth food. She wanted to get a bit of everything, but didn't want to lose character. She settled on toast with butter and jelly, some fruit and a morning tea. She paid for her meal in cash and headed back to the table to join Kevin for breakfast.

"Thank you so much," she said.

"Oh you're welcome."

"You mind if I sit here and join you?"

"Actually, I'm getting ready to head back," Kevin said, while getting ready to stand up.

"Oh would you mind staying for a little while," she asked. "I could use the company." "Kevin felt he should get back to check on Erin and Audrey, but decided to sit a few minutes with the woman. She seemed to have a light breakfast and he didn't think it would take long.

He checked his watch. "I guess I could sit for a few minutes," he said.

"That's all I need," Mattie said. "You sure you don't want anything to eat?"

For the next twenty minutes they talked about Erin and Mattie's volunteer work at the hospital. When he mentioned he was a lawyer she asked if he could help her in her legal push for the hospital to upgrade some of its wards. He gave her a card and suggested she call the office.

"That is a noble thing you're pushing for," he said. "I really need to get back. It was great talking to you," he said. Kevin stood up and folded his paper.

"Oh you too Kevin and I hope Erin gets better," she reached into her bag. "One last thing, would you sign my petition for the cause. I've already collected a few names."

"Sure," Kevin reached into his pocket and pulled out a pen. No matter how many times he tried, the ink would not flow.

"Oh I have a pen," she said. "She reached into her bag and pulled out a weird metal ball point.

"Thanks," he said and signed his name in the weird red ink. The only red signature on the page.

CHAPTER 31

"You have only a short while," said the guard as Aalon entered into the visitors' booth.

"There he is," said Athyna excitedly. She ran to hug him but was immediately restrained by the guards.

"There is no contact." He said. Athyna gave the guard a stare and put her hands down.

"It's okay," Aalon said. "I miss you too." He sat down.

"Aalon, this is Erin."

He looked at me with disappointment. "I am thinking this is a bad idea. This is what or should I say who you had in mind?"

"Aalon, do not lose hope," Athyna said. "We can win."

Athyna gave me a nod to sit down.

"Athyna she is human!" His eyes focused on my face, occasionally looking down at me as if I were beneath him or unfit to represent him. He looked at me and continued. "She's imperfect. She's –"

"Unpredictable," Athyna said. "And most importantly she is your only hope."

There was a moment of silence between the two. It's been a while since I've been in the position of having to defend my service. It was awkward and I honestly could say I wasn't offended. I understand his thinking; I mean there was a lot of risk here.

"Hi," I said as I grabbed Aalon's hand. "Aalon, I know this is not the best of circumstances for us to meet. But I want to help. This has been an experience unlike any other, but I'm confident I can overcome, we can overcome this challenge."

He just listened.

"Since time is not on our side. Why don't you set aside your doubt and just tell me exactly what happened."

He looked at Athyna who gave an encouraging nod. The guards who were standing only a few feet behind him leaned closer.

"Do you mind?" I said. "I believe I do have the right to provide counsel in private."

They stepped back. One of them gave me a less than friendly look.

"Sean was a hurtful person." He started. "He lived a life that was far from pleasing to God. He was born into a life of hardship. He sided with rift raft and criminals, and yes I felt frustration with his decisions, but he was my human to protect and I cared for him. I was responsible for watching, advising and protecting him, -- for guarding him.

I just nodded and listened. Similar to any other client I represented, this was the part where I let them do all the much needed talking.

"As a guardian, you're always on post. Never a moment to turn your back. Unseen dangers are existent almost always. With Sean, however, I worked all the time. He was constantly in the presence of danger. I protected him through fights, ambushes and - "

"Protect how?" I interrupted.

He paused looked at Athyna and then continued.

"We guardians protect in a variety of ways. Conscious, health, anatomy, sleep, physical contact." I just sat there with a confused look on my face. He must have read it and decided to explain. He held up one finger.

"Conscious. Sometimes, when a human is going somewhere or with someone that could lead to something disastrous, we give them what you might refer to as second thoughts, cold feet, or doubt. If we need to really push them to reconsider a decision, we can work with the human anatomy and give that feeling in the pit of their stomach. Sometimes it makes them sick. Other times it's just enough to make them so uncomfortable they change their mind.

"Go on," I encouraged. He held up the third finger.

"Sleep. Well, that's just self-explanatory," he said. "You ever have a deep sleep? The kind where you didn't hear your phone ring, or didn't hear the knock at the door? Sometimes the sleep can last a few minutes or a few hours. Whatever it takes to take you out of the equation. Do you know how many times I've helped save lives just by allowing someone to oversleep by five minutes?" He pushed my shoulder. "Another is through physical contact." "You're on your way somewhere and need to slow down a few seconds to avoid a collision. You may stumble, drop your car keys or fiddle with your car door which can delay you for an appropriate length of time."

"I understand," I said. I was impressed with the information as well as the methods. To think all those times, I just thought I was clumsy. "So what happened to Sean?"

"He lived in a five story apartment in West London with his girlfriend. He was going to murder her, because she wanted to leave him," he said. "I tried to give him doubts. I tried to slow him down. It was already determined in his mind."

He looked at me with sadness in his eyes. His description became frustrated and choppy.

"Sean had a gun. His girlfriend was packing her bags. He begged her to stay. She continued and walked toward the hallway outside of the front door. He followed and aimed. He was going to kill her." He cried into his hands. "Oh God, he was going to kill her."

"What happened?" I pressed.

"I nudged him. That's all I did. I tried to make him stumble. He fell backwards over the stair rail and broke his neck to instant death. I chose to help save his girlfriend and he died for it," he turned and cried into Athyna's shoulder. "He died for it."

"I understand," I replied. "I want to help."

"What can you do?" he asked while looking at me and Athyna. "What can any of you do?"

"Time," said one of the guards who pulled Aalon by his shoulder.

"What can you do?" he repeated again and was led back to the dark shadow.

"I can win," I answered. "Have faith."

"That's for your kind," he said. The doors drew to a close.

I sat there and reflected on his words. Athyna was right. I didn't need to take any notes. Everything he said I retained.

"That is for your kind?" I asked myself in a whisper.

"It's hard to explain," said Athyna who overheard me.

"You call any of this easy to comprehend?" I asked while gesturing toward my new heavenly surroundings.

"Faith is about action based on belief," Athyna responded. "As an angel, what's there to believe?"

"Huh?"

"We see the face of God. We know of his existence. There's nothing to believe. There's just reality."

"So you're saying because you see, there's no reason to believe?"

"No, not because we see, because we know. We experience."

EVEN *Angels* NEED MIRACLES

CHAPTER 32

Kevin waited for the elevator to head back up and see Erin. When it opened, two men stepped out with attitude.

"There he is, one said and pulled him by his jacket, toward the wall. You've got a hearing to attend," one of the men said. "My man Antonio is paying good money for your service."

Kevin pushed the guy grabbing his jacket away, "Look guys, I don't know what you think this is, but I need some time. Call the office and I'm sure they will-"

"You need some time? Look this guy doesn't get it. I knew this lawyer was a bust. Let's just get another one. He pulled out a gun and pushed it to Kevin's temple. Kevin tried to push the man away but was overpowered.

"Help!"

"No you don't!" Mattie yelled as she approached the elevators. "I need him! He's mine!"

The next thing Kevin heard was the screams and pleas of the two guys before he blacked out.

EVEN *Angels* NEED MIRACLES

CHAPTER 33

As I sat at the desk across from my bed, over and over again, I wanted to focus on what happened and who was really responsible, but that was secondary. The issue at hand was whether Aalon deserved his fate, not who was guilty of the crime. I tried to go over my mental notes again, but could not set aside my thoughts on what was happening back home outside of heaven. Although there was something telling me everything back at home was alright, I couldn't help but think about what was going on. How was Audrey? How was Kevin? There was no way for me to concentrate on what I was here to do. The last time I felt this overwhelmed by my thoughts was when my grandmother passed away, years ago. It was strange to have her with me in the same room, looking better than ever.

"You seem bothered," she said as she sat down next to me. "This all just seems too much like a cartoon," I said.

"Oh I know. What do you think it was like for me," she gestured. "One moment, I'm lying in pain, thinking about you and then the next moment I'm more comfortable and at peace than I've ever been. I still do think about you though," she said.

"So you're happy," I asked.

"Baby, I'm full of joy," she said. "So don't worry about me and please don't be sad. All is very well."

"That's good to hear grandma," I said. "Very good."

I decided I would sit outside a little. Perhaps I'll think more clearly and rehearse everything I've recently learned. I walked until I reached a park with a beautiful stream, unfamiliar fruit lined trees and peaceful animals, I sat on a marble-type bench and pondered the whole situation.

"Take a bite of this," said the voice behind me. I turned around to find Iblis standing with some strange fruit in hand. "The last person I offered fruit, said it was a life-changing experience," he said laughing.

I stood up in complete startlement.

"Relax, I'm just here to talk," he said. "Sorry for the show I put on earlier, I just get a little frazzled when angels are around, with their trying to be perfect and pleasing. It's vile if you ask me."

"What do you want?" I asked.

"Just wanted to commend you," he said. "You must be extremely impressive to have been chosen for counsel. I mean to think, an angel calling on the help of a human."

I just sat there listening.

"Let's see, if I recall correctly you've had a record number of court case victories, dozens of offers from firms across the country to join their enterprise, not including Hoffman and Dudley," he said while smiling in my face. "You know, Kevin finds you to be among the best"

"How do you know Kevin?"

"Erin, I'm surprised," he said condescendingly. "You're about to go up against the best arguer and researcher of all time, if you think you've been in tough cases before, you're about to get a lesson in tough. Aalon is as good as mine and as a matter of fact so is all of heaven."

"Erin,!" A distant voice cried out. It was Athyna. She walked toward me.

"We'll see each other again." Iblis said and then disappeared.

"Was that –"

"Yes."

"Are you okay? Did he –"

"He didn't do anything." I said. "Just trying to give me doubt and it's working."

"Come, you mustn't let him get to you."

"Are you serious? I asked. We're talking about the Prince of Darkness."

"He's not without weakness and faults," Athyna said. "He's always believed he's God's equal and so far from it."

Athyna shared a few stories about Iblis and his shortcomings that I didn't know of. It helped to diminished any intimidation that I felt, but I still doubted if I had enough time to prepare.

"All rise," the angel in the purple robe said as the council entered the courtroom. Rather than have seats, they all stood behind separate lecterns that resembled those seen in most church pulpits. They all stood upright in perfect posture. "You may all be seated."

I stood there mesmerized by the vast number of angels in attendance. There were tens of thousands. It sort of reminded me as if we were at a stadium event. The room was set in an oval fashion with the 12 member angelic council surrounding half of the perimeter. Their huge lecterns sat much higher than the courtroom floor, which gave the room a sense of their authority. Each council member had a distinguished look, some had what appeared to be a serious disposition, some looked compassionate; all of them looked as if they were prepared to listen intently. I didn't see any tools for note taking on any of the lecterns. There were, however, recording angels floating on each side of the room high above all of us, including the council members. Each recording angle faced the center of the room, where the accusing side and the defense sat in the center of the floor facing what appeared to be the leading member of the council. Aalon sat in a lone seat, in front of the council in perfect view.

"You'll do fine," Athyna whispered.

"I don't know," I said. "This is just way over my head."

An angel in the council fixed his eyes on me, "Shhhh." "It is time to receive the adversary."

The doors swung open as Iblis walked into the room. He had two assistants with hooded robes following. He evenly switched his focus from the council to me. He looked as cunning as ever. One of his assistants handed him a scroll. As he made his way to the presenting table he gestured for his assistants to be seated.

"Who are they?" I whispered.

"Probably fallens that haven't the courage to show their face. As long as they aren't presenting they can remain with their hoods."

"Members of the council," Iblis said, while staring at Athyna. "Are you going to allow her outbursts? Isn't this the place with all the rules?"

"You must refrain from talking," the angel reminded me. "Your full silence is expected." He looked at Athyna with a most penetrating stare. "Our apologies," I said. I made sure to not make any more interruptions.

"We will hear from the accusing side."

"Thank you," Iblis said. "Thank you indeed." Iblis stood up and walked to Aalon.

"Hello Aalon," he said in a soft slithery whisper. "No more comfy quarters for you after this. You're as good as mine."

CHAPTER 34

Audrey woke up and checked her watch. It was 8:30. She felt groggy, given she had to sleep in that stiff recliner all night. She stretched and peered around the room to find Kevin gone. Standing up, she checked Erin's monitors as if she knew what any of the numbers meant. She didn't notice any change. She was sure that Kevin was either getting something to eat or on his phone in the lobby. She was confident he would be right back.

She walked over to Erin and kissed her on the forehead.

"Hey sis," she whispered. "We're all here, hoping you come on back." Audrey lightly rested her head next to Erin's without disturbing any of the electrodes or tubes. She stared out into the hall when she saw the nurses run by with what looked like Kevin on a wheeled bed.

At first she thought her mind was playing tricks but quickly thought to check it out, since this week was turning out to be so bizarre.

She walked to the hallway and saw Kevin being wheeled into the next room.

"Oh my god," she yelled. "What happened?"

No one answered. Each nurse was occupied with saving his life.

"What happened?" She yelled. There weren't any signs of blood or bruises.

"Ma'am. Are you with him?" One of the nurses asked.

"Yes," Audrey answered, knowing that was the only way to get any answers. His name is Kevin. Kevin Banneker."

We came here together. We were waiting in the room next door, with my sister who was in the accident. Now what happened to him?"

"We're not sure. We think he passed out. Could be stress. Could be diabetic. We're going to have to run tests. Please step out of the room. We'll call you when it's safe to come in."

Audrey could not believe what was happening. She went back into the other room knelt beside the bed as Yvonne came in the room.

Yvonne knelt beside her, "Have faith. It's all going to be okay," she said. She led them both in prayer.

"The bottom line is Aalon placed his concern over another human, over the care he should have had for his own," Iblis said as he stood in front of the council. His speaking level was raised more for effect than concern. Aalon looked deeply worried.

"In this trial, I plan to show just how Aalon allowed his own personal prejudices and bias get the best of him and for that a human lost his life and soul. I ask that you find him guilty."

He turned to his seat and sat down. I thought he would never shut up. Iblis definitely gave the longest opening statement I've yet to hear. The only thing that bothered me was that it was very good.

He looked at me and blew into his finger as if it were a smoking gun.

I stood up to give my remarks. I didn't know whether to start off with ladies and gentlemen or what. I cleared my throat.

"Members of the angelic council, what we have in front of us today is a case that is founded on a grave mistake. What the accuser would suggest is Aalon the guardian purposely set out to end the life of his human assignment, of Sean

Logan. This is preposterous. Many of us have made mistakes before and though we pay for those mistakes in all cases, the punishment should fit the violation." I looked at the council in the most assertive manner I could. A few members looked at each other. I also looked at Aalon, whose worried face did not go away. I made sure to make as much eye contact as I could with each council member. Since they sat in a semi-circular fashion, there was an unusual almost 180 degree arching presentation I had to quickly adjust to make sure my attention was given equally. Though it was the high ranking council member who received a bit more of my focus.

"In the short time I've had to survey, question, and study all the facts of this case, in the short time I've had to research the history of this angel, and in the short time I've had to speak to those that know Aalon longer than I've been in existence. I've discovered that the admirable character traits that are intensely rooted in this angel are not found in many. Committed, disciplined, humble," I turned to him as I spoke. "It was he who brought himself before the council in the first place. He's loyal. He's honest, even when he himself faces punishment. He's dependable, obedient, and upright. He's many things. I can list forever all the elements that make up his being and though as much as I'd like to, the one thing I will not be able to say is he's perfect." A few of the council members looked at Aalon. The majority focused on me.

"I want to ask the court to consider the incident as well as the intent of this angel. I want the court to recognize the heart of Aalon as much as the facts of the case, because of his compassion, his love and care for Sean and his character is as much of a factual part as anything else that will be presented." As I spoke I read the expressions of a few council members and a few spectators, but the one expression that perplexed me and had me most concerned was the sinister smile of Iblis as he followed my every word and my every motion.

My opening was nowhere as lengthy as Iblis', but it was long enough to make my throat dry. As I wrapped up my statement, I sat down and hoped I didn't stutter too much or give off a rough opening statement than it appeared to myself.

I craved the water that Athyna gave to me. "That was both impassioned and eloquent," she whispered.

"Great," I said. "But I was going for effective."

CHAPTER 35

Audrey sat in earnest prayer. It seemed like her world was caught in a whirlpool and she was the only person on board the life raft. The recent activities that occurred within the last few days really pushed her into a conversation with God that was entirely overdue. No longer, did she see herself as the center of concern. She realized that there were other things more important than money or her own worries. This was a wakeup call that she would have never anticipated or would soon forget.

CHAPTER 36

I silently cleared my throat as I stood from my chair. Iblis finished grilling a character witness that ended up making Aalon look like the devil himself. "Are guardians expected to always be on watch of their assignment? Are guardians responsible for the well being of their assignment?" Should a guardian be accountable for harm that comes to their assignment? Every answer ended in yes. Now it was my turn to put things in greater perspective. Isriahel, another guardian who considers Aalon one of his closest friends stared at me. It was obvious he was fascinated that I was here in heaven.

"Hello Isriahel," he shook his head silently in amazement and responded, "Hello."

"Do you think Aalon purposely let harm come to Sean?"

"No, Aalon would never do that. I know him well." He turned to Aalon and smiled with a slight nod.

"How would you describe Aalon's work ethic?"

"Top of the line. He's considered wise beyond his years and often tells others of ways to improve their devotion."

I went on to ask Isriahel other questions to prove Aalon was not this killer Iblis tried to paint him as. At the end of my questioning, I felt pretty good about our responses.

As I was about to sit down, I noticed one of Iblis' assistants whispering something into his ear. He smiled.

"A cross examination?" One of the the council members asked.

"Just one question," Iblis responded. He stood up and leaned toward Isriahiel "Isriahel, I know that being a guardian must be a pretty personal journey, with all the closeness you experience with your assignment. But just answer me this. Has Aalon ever expressed frustration with his assignment?

Isriahel paused. Everyone could tell he didn't want to answer, which is what Iblis wanted. "Ah hesitation," he said. "Let me rephrase. How frequent did Aalon expressed frustration about Sean."

Isriahel looked at Aalon and said softly, "often."

"Let the council record, even Aalon's closest of companions recall him being frustrated with his assignment," he said as he sat down.

The lead angel from the council turned to Iblis, "Any more questions," he asked.

"No, I'm finished with this one." He turned to me and smiled. I held the stare for a few seconds and looked away.

"Very well, we will meet back on the new day."

Iblis walked over to me as the other angels began to disperse. Athyna and Jericho stood as he extended his hand.

"Good first day Erin," he said. I refused to shake hands with him. "If she is the best you have, you've already lost." He turned, looked at his assistants and walked away. He walked toward Aalon and whispered something before walking out of the room with his demons.

I stood up. I felt more than a bit shaken of the day's outcome. Athyna and Jericho did their best to give me encouragement, but I couldn't hear anything they said. I slowly walked to Aalon who was being shackled to be taken back.

"What did he say to you?" I asked.

Aalon looked at me and with brief pause answered, "He said my fate would be better if I just choose to be a fallen."

"Have faith." I said.

"That's all I have left," he said while being escorted away.

CHAPTER 37

Lorna hung limply. The pain had gone on so long, screams nor any sound for that matter could not escape her. If only she would fade away. She welcomed death and nothingness.

"You are a fool of fools," Furcus said. His grin was full of pleasure. As a fallen, he escaped his own torture in exchange for delivering a litany of angels to the cause of Iblis. He was an untouched torturer – the only in hell. His position was the one that every captured being envied. The only position that was not tortured or harmed, but lived almost as good as Iblis himself. Lorna's former position was a close second. "You dare to betray your own comforts here? I'm going to love making you hate this."

She could barely respond. She resented her leading Aalon to the library almost as soon as she left him to his search. Lorna would indeed suffer for her involvement. The penalty for sharing hope was torture with no rest. Perhaps it was intended all along for her to fail and end up in these very chains.

It seemed that the wall where she was stretched by the wrists and ankles started to grow taller and wider, expanding her body to unknown limits. Although she was in spiritual form, it was as if she had been given flesh just to experience such pain. The walls began to get warm, then hot and hotter still. Soon the walls became hot coals slowly cooking her flesh. Just when she thought there was no more life inside, a scream that she never could have conjured, shot out of her. She wished that she hung in this position with at least her back against the wall. There would be no end to this punishment – ever.

CHAPTER 38

Yesterday's session did not go well and it seemed that today's wasn't fairing any better. Iblis stitched a sound argument bashing Aalon's decision to physically interfere with his assignment to ensure the well being of another. Witness after witness, it seemed the cards were becoming more stacked against our defense.

"Your honor, I call Laylah, another guardian to whom Aalon was close," Iblis said. "Perhaps she can further reveal the dishonor in Aalon's actions."

In the chair only a few feet away to the left of Aalon, slowly appeared a female angel. She looked around the room and noticed Aalon. The sadness in her eyes was telling of her concern for Aalon.

"Laylah, this way. This way," Iblis said while snapping to get her attention.

The head council member explained to Laylah the trial situation and requested her full cooperation regarding her response to the questions she would face. She agreed to comply. After much intense questioning on her background and the relationship she's had with her humans, he finally got to the matter.

"So, as you stated a guardian is to always put the well-being of the assignment into consideration; then you would have to say that an angel who puts another as priority is committing a violation."

"In some cases, in most cases – the human who is planning to bring harm to themselves or others is opposed by their guardian. It's not wrong for me to oppose my human from hurting another, because in hurting others, they bring judgment and wrath upon themselves."

"But when is it okay to kill your assignment?"

"Objection," I said sharply. Iblis rephrased the question.

"Is it okay for an angel to allow the life of an assignment to end before time?"

"I would imagine no," Layla responded.

"You would imagine? You would imagine?" Iblis grew angry with her answer. "Fact, Aalon shared with many his frustration with his assignment. Fact, he CHOSE to have more concern for his assignment's girlfriend rather than his assignment. Aalon should be held responsible. He took the life of the one he's assigned to protect. To me it's the most horrid act ever committed by any angel. EVER! I ask you again. Is it okay for an angel –"

"No!" Layla sobbed. "No! I'm sorry Aalon. I'm so sorry."

Iblis turned to look at Aalon. "I'm finished with my questioning." He shook his head and laughed to himself before returning to his seat. Seconds later a thought came across his mind. He leaned back to whisper in one of his assistant's hooded ears.

The lead council member held his hand up to pause and give Layla time to regain her composure. I slowly walked to her and handed her a cloth to wipe her eyes.

"Layla, have you ever made a mistake as a guardian?"

She paused. "Of course. I learn about my assignment every day. I can't predict her actions with 100 percent accuracy."

"What about interaction from other guardians? I mean, people are with people every day. So I assume that while their guardian angels are with them, there must be in some cases a room full of guardian angels, each guarding their own assignment. Am I right?"

"Of course, but"

"But what?"

"There is not much dialogue. We are responsible for keeping a watchful eye – like you said – on our individual assignments. The slightest distraction can throw us off."

"I see. So is it ever practiced that an angel would protect the assignment of another?"

"Not that I can recall," she said. "We are all assigned our own human."

"It must be allowed sometime, right?"

"Members of the council, she's answered the question." Iblis said with an interruption. "It doesn't happen!"

I ignored him and started to turn to my seat. "Just one more question."

"Sure," she said.

"Who's watching your assignment now?" I paused as whispers started to flutter throughout the room. "I mean you're here, and if I'm not mistaking you can't be at more than one place at once, right?"

"Right," she said. "I was summoned here and had to come. I was always told that whenever we're summoned to heaven that takes priority. I believe there is another guardian that looks after our assignments temporarily, until we return."

"So there are times, when a guardian can intervene on another's behalf."

"I guess so," she said.

"No further questions."

Iblis looked at me in disgust. I sat down and poured myself a drink of water.

He stood up almost in spite, "One cross," he said.

"You may," the head council said.

"Layla, for another guardian to intervene it has to be ordained from heaven, correct?" He said. "Another angel cannot decide on his own terms who to protect?"

"I guess so." She said.

"There you go again," he lashed out. "Am I correct or you guess so?"

"Correct," She said.

"No further questions."

The head council member looked to see if I had a response. I didn't. He dismissed Layla and in an instant she vanished. I needed to turn this train around and I was running out of time.

"We will adjourn until the new day," the presiding council member said. Every angel arose and began to depart. I turned to Iblis to see if he would make his way over to antagonize me. Instead, I saw his assistant whisper in his ear, something that apparently caused him to become angry, and in a flash they all disappeared.

CHAPTER 39

Audrey continued to read her Bible as she sat in the quite room.

"You should try reading the book of Luke," the nun said as she walked in. She had a grandmother kind of quality, a little seasoned but still with enough pep in her step to show she's still got a lot to offer. "He was a doctor who recorded in great detail, the healings of Jesus."

Audrey just nodded and smiled.

"You know, I've seen you here several days straight. Why don't you go home to rest one day. She'll receive good care." She said, while quietly brushing her hair from Erin's face

"I can't," she said. "I need to be here."

"I understand," the nun said. "It's just I don't want to see you worry yourself sick. It happens you know." She walked over to Audrey and gave her a hug. "It's in God's hands."

Just then a doctor walked in. He read the chart on the bed.

"There she is," he whispered. "Oh, I'm sorry, I'm Doctor Dan." They shook his hand.

"Who are you again," Sister Mary asked.

"I'm Doctor Dan." He walked over to look at the monitors and saw Audrey's opened Bible on the chair. He mistakenly knocked it to the floor and put it back on the chair closed.

"I don't know any Doctor Dan," she said. "Are you new to intensive care?"

"Why yes I'm am," he responded.

"Well, I am Sister Mary McCray. I'm just making my visiting rounds. I'll be back in a few minutes," she turned to whisper to Audrey. "Child, you buzz the nurse if anything unusual happens. Anything unusual, you hear?"

"Uh yes sister."

"See you two later."

"Peace be with you Doctor Dan," she said.

"Huh?" he said staring at Erin. He turned to give the nurse his attention.

"Never mind," she said and she left.

CHAPTER 40

I had more trouble sleeping than any time before. I felt so much rested on my shoulders. I did my best to have faith and believe in myself, but it seemed as if Athyna and Jericho had more confidence in me than I had in myself. I was relieved when sleep finally fell upon me and took pleasure in dreaming about normal times.

"I have to journey to Earth," Jericho said to Athyna as she sat outside of Erin's room. Athyna in almost motherly fashion shushed Jericho from speaking too loudly. She was glad to know Erin rested. She marveled at Erin's courage and tenacity. She knew she'd contacted the right human for the job.

"Is everything okay? What takes you there," she asked.

"Just going to go check on Erin. Want to make sure she's okay."

Athyna could tell Jericho wasn't saying everything he knew, but she trusted him. "Can I help," she asked.

"I'll be fine. Stay with her here. She may need you."

He gave her a hug and left.

Sean moaned as his tormentor took a breather from beating him. He did not know pain could be so intense. While his body ached, his throat was equally as sore from screaming. There was no getting used to the treatment. His tormentor, after stretching, leaned back to give another slash across his back, but before he could continue in his full swing, Aalon's hand caught the strap.

"You can't save him here," the demon said. He threw Aalon down and threatened to beat him. "You should take pleasure in knowing you can't be touched – for now."

He laughed and struck Sean again while staring at Aalon. He hit him again and again. Aalon sat helplessly sobbing as Sean screamed and begged the demon to stop, as well as for forgiveness from God.

"Take him back to his quarters," Iblis said instructing the two demons who grabbed Aalon by the arms and dragged him out of the room. "I might not be able to torture you, but this should be plenty of pain," Iblis yelled. He turned to Sean and struck him with all his might.

CHAPTER 41

Jericho signed the visitor's registration. While he knew Erin's heavenly body was in good hands with Athyna he knew it was still just as important to make sure the Earthly body was receiving good care. When Sister Mary whispered a prayer about her concern for Erin, he knew he had to see for himself. Jericho had relationships with several humans on Earth – a janitor in Iowa, a Shepherd in Eritrea East Africa, an artist in Ecquador and Baltimore's Sister Mary was one who he always made time to visit. She didn't know he was an angel, but she knew there was something about him that was different and godly. He was looking forward to seeing her again.

Sister Mary met Jericho a few years back. He rescued her from a mugging near her home. A few years before that, he returned her lost dog to her home. And a few months before that, she gave him a donation while he sat begging outside at a corner. She gave him what little money she could afford and held a conversation with him while splitting her lunch at a bus stop. She told him how different he was compared to other less fortunate people she met.

He'll never forget what she said to him.

"You're not one of us are you," she asked. He paused trying to find the right response. He couldn't lie to her. "It's okay, don't say anything else. Do what you're supposed to do. I'm a believer you know. I know your kind walk among us and I won't pry or make it any more difficult for you. She got on her bus when it pulled up and smiled at him through the window. He was sure she knew, and it wasn't a problem as long as neither of them talked in specific terms. He was okay with it and though they saw each other rarely and for short spans of time, Sister Mary became one of the closest friend he had on Earth.

Little did he know how much she would have appreciated his presence some 50 years ago, when she was merely a teenager. She and her sister lived with her mother and her mom's boyfriend – a woman beating deadbeat, who forced Mary and her young nine year-old sister to commit lewd acts while her mother was away at work. Sister Mary was too afraid too tell. Her mother's boyfriend continued to molest her and her sister Monica for years until she could no longer accept the abuse and Monica ultimately committed suicide. Mary has never forgiven herself for her cowardice.

Jericho adjusted his blazer jacket. Normally, when he made an Earth visit, he didn't care too much about his attire. Seldom did an angel really care about what people thought of them – especially when it came to their appearance. This time though, he didn't want to draw any attention toward himself. His normal meek attire, long beard and worn shoes made people stare for a short while, and then repulsed by his status, they paid almost no attention to him at all. He liked that. He enjoyed being able to operate with a slim chance of someone discovering the miracles around him better than with every eye drawn toward his direction. Today, however he wanted to visit Erin's comatose body at the hospital. He knew that if he didn't at least look presentable he'd have a few challenges even getting into the building, let alone the room.

As he walked toward the elevator, he saw himself in the mirror, his clean shave; nicely fitted clothes and polished loafers gave him the feeling that he was as much a part of the human world as the next man.

"Hello," said the doctor on the elevator.

Jericho smiled before responding, "Hello, would you mind pressing five please?"

"You bet."

When he got to the intensive care ward, he walked past the receptionist as if she never saw him.

"Jerry, is that you," Sister Mary asked. She walked over and gave him a hug. I bet you thought I wouldn't recognize you without your beard.

"Oh, just came to check on that lawyer I heard about. My friend is a client of hers and I wanted to see how she's doing."

"What a coincidence," Sister Mary said. Her tone was hard to place, almost as if she knew there was more to his visit than he let on. "Well, she's in room 523. I can lead you if you like."

"That would be fine," he said. They made their way to the room to find Audrey asleep in the recliner with the Bible closed on her lap. Dr. Dan was leaning over Erin whispering in her ear.

"What are you doing?" Sister Mary interrupted.

Jericho gently stepped in front of her.

"Jericho!" Dr. Darren said in an almost slithery fashion. "He pushed away from Erin and changed, losing his human form and turning into the fallen angel Geragan.

From out of thin air, Jericho drew a sword and time came to a still. He never knew how far time ceased to move, whether it was the universe, planet, or just that isolated area, but one thing was certain, nothing in that hospital showed any signs of movement or cognition. He swung mightily making sure to not destroy the room. "Back to hell you go," Jericho commanded. His blade barely missed.

Geragan picked Jericho up by his shirt and threw him into the hall. Jericho stood up as Geragan leaped into the air to pounce. Slipping on his back, Jericho held up his sword. In quick-like fashion, however, Geragen floated in mid air so as to not land on the upright blade. He instead swatted the sword from Jericho's hands and landed on top, choking him with all his might.

"One of us will die today," Geragan said. "Today is your day." Jericho's body began to fade as Geragan's grip grew more forceful. He tried to push Geragan off, but he couldn't get the leverage. Sister Mary, did not know how she could come to see this, but it was as clear to her as if two humans were fighting in front of her. She walked to Jericho's sword and tried lifting it, but it was too heavy.

"Please God!" she yelled. As she continued to struggle with the sword. A soft hand touched her shoulder. She turned around to find another angel behind her. The angel bent to grab the sword and speared Geragan in the center of his back and then pulled it out and swung cleanly at his neck, bringing Geragan to his demise.

"Thank you Hanna," Jericho said as he stood to his feet.

"It is quite all right," Hanna said bowing slightly. She went back to Erin's side and stood guard and then faded before Sister Mary and Jericho's eyes. He wasn't sure why Sister Mary could see all that took place.

He gently gave her a hug, while she prayed.

"I was right about you," she declared.

"Sister Mary, you were not supposed to see any of that. How are you?"

"I'm well," she said. "I know you have to go. I'm fine. How's Erin?"

Jericho walked to Erin and looked her over. "She's fine. You did well to question that doctor," he said. "But you're right. I do have to leave. Will you let Audrey know Erin is fine."

"I will pass the message, Jericho," she said. "Will you pass a message on for me too?"

"Your sister said she doesn't blame you. She loves you," Jericho paused. He slowly walked to her, gently took her hands in his and pulled her into a hug, "and God loves you too."

Nearly 50 years of hurt and sadness was finally lifted off her heart. She cried uncontrollably as Earth stood still. Jericho was determined to hold her for as long as he could. "It's time you you finally let it go," he said softly.

Sister Mary's eyes continued to well up. Her old frame grew tired as she made her way back to sit down on the chair next to Audrey. She took the Bible into her hands tightly and began to sing a gospel hymn. Jericho walked out of the room and faded away just as Earth jolted back to time.

CHAPTER 42

"I think this is a big mistake," I whispered to Athyna. "There's nothing to gain by having him here."

"I explained it to Aalon, but it's what he wants for whatever reason. I've already requested."

"Do you want to do this," I questioned Athyna. I was upset that she and Aalon discussed who should be called to the stand with out me.

"No," she responded.

"Then let me do my job!"

The lead council member spoke over us.

"Sean Logan, please take the stand."

In seconds a bloodied and battered Sean appeared on stand. His scars and disfiguration began to heal on site. Apparently Aalon took pleasure in having him away from his ordeal for at least a short while. Sean looked around to take in his new surroundings. Iblis, obviously angered that Sean was not in some sort of demonic torture device was not one to give time for adjustments. He quickly began his questioning.

"Sean, good to see you again."

Sean jumped back in total alarm. We can only imagine what kind of fearful thoughts ran through his head. Iblis was enjoying the response and kept on getting closer and closer. Sean looked like a helpless child. It was hard to imagine him as this tough specimen that Aalon described.

The head council did not show any sign of understanding or compassion.

"Sean, you need to restrain yourself. You're here for a series of questions. Do you understand?"

Sean just stared. The situation was just too overwhelming. In the flesh world, he would have fainted; here however, he developed a nervous shake. Aalon, who had seen enough, stood up from his seat and walked over to him.

"Objection!" Iblis yelled. "Objection. Would someone restrain him?"

No one moved. We all watched as he approached the center and calmly placed his hand on Sean's hand, bringing him a wave of comfort and ease.

Sean just stared. He seemed like he comprehended. Their eyes met and held as if two long lost brothers met for the first time. Aalon was immediately escorted back to his seat.

"Sean, this won't be long. I'll ask you a few questions and then you can go back to where you were." Iblis said laughing. "My dear Sean, do you know why you are a guest in my house?" Before Sean could answer, Iblis Interrupted. "Let me clarify that. Don't get me wrong you were on the list anyway. You've got a track record that certainly makes me proud and I welcome you home, but did you know you are here, and spending eternity in hell truly because of an untimely death?"

Sean sat there, his tears began to fall. He stared at Iblis and back at Aalon. I wanted to interrupt. It seemed like this was nothing more than rubbing salt in his already exposed wounds.

"I shouldn't be here?" Sean asked. "Please, I'm sorry for what I've done. If I could have a second chance?"

"Oh come, come," Iblis said teasingly. "We're not here for that. You belong to me. I just wanted you to know you were destined for hell. After all your own guardian angel set you up."

"Objection."

"Sustained."

"I just call it as I see it, dear council members," Iblis said. "But I'll withdraw."

Iblis went on to grill Sean with questions concerning his lifestyle. He slanted all of his responses and tried to convince Sean to believe it was his questionable lifestyle that frustrated Aalon in wanting to kill him. It was an absurd notion that received many objections and several outbursts from Aalon but I have to admit it was laid out pretty convincingly.

"Who or what do you blame for your being here?" Iblis said.

Sean seemed confused. He didn't know how to answer the question or he didn't want to answer the question. "Do you blame your lifestyle or Aalon?"

"Objection. Who he blames is irrelevant."

"Your honor, I'm trying to establish whether or not even his assignment blames him for the circumstances."

"I don't like the way that question is framed," the head council member said. "Unless you-"

"Very well, Sean do you blame Aalon for your death." Iblis quickly interrupted the council member with his question.

He looked at me and then Aalon.

"Yes I do."

"No further questions."

EVEN *Angels* NEED MIRACLES

CHAPTER 43

Audrey finally woke up from her sleep. It was the first night she slept fully. She woke up to see Sister Mary sitting on the chair reading the Bible.

"Good morning," Audrey said. "How long have you been here?"

"Oh, long enough, I've been visiting between you and your friend. I convinced the nurses to move him to the same room if possible. They said perhaps sometime this afternoon. I hope you don't mind."

"That was very kind for you to do," Audrey said. She stood up to stretch. Despite her sleeping throughout the night, it was on a recliner and wasn't the most comfortable. She had no recall of any of the spiritual events that took place. "Thank you."

Audrey walked to Erin and held her hand.

"She'll be fine dear. Have faith." Sister Mary said tenderly.

"How are you so sure?"

"An angel told me."

I slowly stood up. The tension in the room was thick. Sean set us back even more than I expected. Nothing I would be able to get out of him would help us. There wasn't a being present who wasn't expecting something dramatic to happen. I had to let him go. I chickened out.

"No questions for me at this time," I said, my voice started to break. I could only imagine what Aalon must have felt, to see Sean have to go back. It must have been heavy on his heart. Quite honestly, it was too much for me as well. "May I ask for a recess?"

"What are you doing?" Athyna whispered.

The truth was prolonging the inevitable. I could not stand the position I was put in.

"Well, since there are no more witnesses Erin, please be ready at the 10th chime to deliver your closing remark."

"This ought to be good," Iblis said in a loud whisper. I just ignored him.

The head council member hit the gavel and everyone started to adjourn. I walked out quickly. I needed some time to myself and I didn't want anyone to see me cry.

"Erin, I'll join you," Athyna yelled.

"Thank you." I turned to Athyna. "But I need to be alone."

Out of the corner of my eye, I could see Iblis was upset by my need for a sudden break. Aalon looked like he was in total shock. I walked out of the courtroom and made sure to not make direct eye contact with him or anyone else.

I entered the garden Athyna showed me earlier and sat down on the bench. As angels walked by, I could feel them staring in an almost disappointed manner. Why couldn't they take care of their own problem, I thought. Here they are with all this power and they choose me to come to save the day. I can't do this.

"What are you staring at," I yelled. My tears began to flow and I didn't care.

"They're probably admiring your courage Erin," I turned around to find Aalon standing behind me. "Do you mind if I join you?"

"I'd like to be alone," I said.

"Sure," he said. "But you can have this. It's clean, trust me."

I took the cloth as he started to walk away.

"No wait," I said. "How did you manage to come out here, and what do you mean courage?"

Aalon turned around and walked back toward me. He knelt down, took my hand as he stared into my eyes. "First, I told the guards I needed to speak to my lawyer. Erin, look what you have accomplished. You were asked to leave your familiar setting and believe in something that until now could only be considered impossible," my eyes continued to flow with tears. "I was wrong to look down on you. I was wrong to judge you. Your faith has reminded me that I must look deeper. I must look past my own ability to see. That's what I mean by your courage."

He gently took the cloth from me and wiped my eyes.

"I don't want you to suffer because of me" I gasped. I immediately hugged him. He held me and gently rocked. The tears flowed even more.

"I guess I should head back," I said. Aalon released me and stood up. "Whatever becomes of this, I'll be okay" he said.

"I don't want to make a mistake," I responded.

"Erin, you make mistakes. I make mistakes. But God doesn't. You're here representing me because he allowed it. Continue to have faith."

"But it just doesn't look good," I wiped my eyes. "Iblis might have this outcome in his control."

"Funny how you used Iblis and control in the same sentence. He has longed for control and power for so long. It's been his chase since time began and I now know, it is also his weakness." Aalon stood up. "Come, we must head back."

Just then I heard a loud chime.

"I will do my best," I said.

He turned to me one last time, while gradually fading away.

"Whatever the outcome, your victory is already in you," He said.

An overwhelming smile took over and I dashed to the courtroom. Stepping through the doors with two chimes to spare.

"You made it back," Iblis said in jest. "Let's get this over with."

I closed my eyes and said a silent prayer. And I remembered what I just learned in the garden,
"He has longed for control and power for so long. It's been his chase since time began and his weakness." A victorious vision appeared before me. I knew what needed to be done.

"Members of the council, I'd like to call Iblis to the stand."

CHAPTER 44

Audrey and Sister Mary moved the chairs out of the way as the nurses wheeled Kevin into the room. They reconnected his machines into the outlets and excused themselves.

Sister Mary said a short prayer.

"Lord please bring them both back," she said. "We are placing our trust and faith in your hands. Amen."

EVEN *Angels* NEED MIRACLES

CHAPTER 45

After the whispers and murmuring and Iblis' shocking outburst, he finally made his way to the stand for questioning. If looks could kill, I'd have been dead a few times.

"Why are you stretching this out," he asked. His nashing teeth only amplified the appearance of his anger.

"I'm asking the questions," I responded. I walked around the room a bit to get my plan together.

"According to the records, you showed up almost immediately after the death. Correct?"

"Yes, what's your point?"

"What was Aalon's reaction like?"

Iblis turned to Aalon and smiled back at me, "He flew away."

"You must be referring to when he left to give his report to the council," I corrected.

"I don't know where he went," he responded. "All I know is he took off from the crime scene like any other murderer I've watched."

"Didn't he try to revive him," I asked.

"Wasn't there for that." He admired his finger nails, while polishing them on his garment.

"Well the records show he spent quite a while trying to revive him," I said. "I would think that shows concern."

"Concern would be to keep an eye on the assignment in your care, and not steal his life in the first place," he interrupted.

I could tell Iblis was not going to let me bring in the real facts of the case without a challenge. I continued with my plan. It was risky, but my only shot. I walked over to Iblis and stared right into his face.

"Isn't it ironic how you could bring such an accusation, with your long history?"

"What do you mean by that?" Iblis followed my every movement. I could tell his confidence was leaving him by the way he slowed down his response time.

"Well it's just that – in the world, you are the biggest stealer and killer of us all --" I started to say.
"WRONG!" he interrupted angrily. "I've never stolen or killed in my existence. Every murder, every misplaced item, every mishap, every sin was not from my doing."

"You do know you're under oath." I said.

"You can't name one murder or one thing I've stolen," He countered. "I am merely the suggester. I've never forced anyone to murder, lie, or steal. Everyone makes their own choice. Aalon deserves to be punished. As much as I would like to take credit for his actions, he did it on his own! I would love to have planted the idea, but even I didn't think of the sheer genius behind a guardian angel killing his assignment."

"But-"

"There is no but!" He stood up and yelled. "I made the mistake of seeing myself as above God and he's never forgiven me. Aalon has ruined the trust between God and humans. If every human is assigned a guardian and even one is killed at their hands the relationship is no longer perfect. Aalon ruined it on his own! He got frustrated. He lost his temper and he killed him. He needs to be punished!"

"Iblis he made a mistake."

"No he did not, ask him! Ask him!"

Iblis stood up from the stand and pointed to Aalon. "You were angry with Sean. Admit it! You saved him over and over again! You helped him! Protected him! And still he wouldn't learn! He wouldn't change! He didn't even say thank you for all those times!"

"Order! Order!" the head angel screamed while pounding his fist in to the lectern.

"You were angry, weren't you! You were furious! ANSWER!!!"

"YES!" Aalon yelled.

Even Iblis looked surprised. His pause showed complete unpreparedness.

"Aalon No!" I yelled.

"You see," he said. Iblis stood from his chair and pointed at the sobbing Aalon. "He admits it. The mistake would be to not punish Aalon. If that is the case then it truly shows this council and GOD himself as playing favorites. He picks and chooses who he saves and who he damns!" Iblis' intensity began to grow again. The foam started to build in the corners of his mouth. His fury was raw and powerful. If I had flesh here, it would certainly be covered in goose bumps. "And ultimately, HE'S UNFIT TO JUDGE ANYONE!!!!"

A deafening silence filled the room as Aalon continue to sob. He stood up and made his way to the front, "I was angry! I was angry, because I cared. I loved him. I wanted the best for him. I wanted him to learn from his mistakes. I am not without emotion. All guardians form a bond and develop sincere hopes for the ones we guard. But murder is a thing of hate and I did not hate him. Angry? Yes. Furious? Yes. Irate? Murderous? Out of control? – NEVER!" A thunderous boom of chatter filled the room, even among the council. Both Iblis and Aalon held a combatative stare with no one backing down. Despite the commotion and exchange, I could see the bigger picture being played. As the head council member banged his gavel. I looked at Iblis in surprise.

"This is not about Aalon," I said to him.

"All of you are fools. This has never been about Aalon." He responded. "Through his representatives, your God has a decision to make and unless it's the right one it's all over. I pray he doesn't punish him, yet if he does, so be it. I'll get another fallen. I will not lose this advantage."

I closed my eyes. My plan was about to be put in action. There would be no turning back. My mouth did not want to form the words, but I forced them out and eliminated any need for closing statements.

"Members of the council, I move to change our plea to guilty."

Iblis looked at me in awe and then stood up and clinched his fist in victory.

"What!" Athyna stood up grabbed my shoulders and turned me to face her.

Aalon, Jericho and everyone else gasped almost in unison. The council members banged their gavels to regain the room's composure.

The demonic guards walked to Aalon carrying the shackles. They salivated and were eager to get him back to hell.

"You do know your guilty plea would send him to hell for eternity," the lead council member asked.

"I do, but given the testimonies that Iblis shared and Sean and the others, what Aalon did is by far the worst misdeed ever."

"I concur!" Iblis shouted.

"He has ruined any possible trust between the protection of God and his flock."

"Indeed, indeed," Iblis said.

"That's far more wrong than seeking power and control,"

"I agree," Iblis said.

"Therefore I am seeking that Aalon be sent to hell," I turned to face Iblis, "as its new Prince of Darkness!"

"What!" Iblis yelled. He stared at me while more commotion filled the room. The council banged their gavels another time to reestablish control.

The demons who were walking toward Aalon dropped their chains in mid stride and turned to me.

"We need order!" The council members yelled.

"I'll kill you!" Iblis said. "He leaped from his stand and landed directly in front of me.

Courtroom guards however grabbed him and placed him in a hold. It took six guards to control him. His rage was even more powerful than when he spoke earlier on the stands. He struggled to free himself but to no avail.

Slowly, the head angel council member stood up ready to give their ruling. A tense hush filled the room as each council member stood one at a time.

"We have heard all testimony and because you have entered a guilty plea, there is no challenge to Iblis' case. It is important for you to know that this ruling will be final,"

It was apparent that Iblis was in fear. He could see his grip on control was starting to slip. I prayed he would take the bait.

He mumbled a few words.

"I'm sorry Iblis, the record needs to record all sayings," the head council member said.

Iblis paused, looked at me and slowly said, "I am withdrawing the charge."

"What was that?" I asked.

"I said I am withdrawing the charge!"

Cheers and dancing filled the room. Aalon fell to his knees as Athyna and Jericho ran to embrace him.

"Not so fast," I said. The cheers started to subside. "You imprisoned Aalon and he suffered for a charge you no longer find him guilty of committing. He needs to be remunerated."

"He gets his freedom, that's all he gets!" Iblis yelled back.

"Members of the council?" I interrupted. I prayed they would see my point.

"Iblis, it is custom to repair the wrong in such a case. I will allow it," the head angel said. "Aalon what do you seek?"

Aalon stood up and slowly walked to Iblis. He stared at him and said, "I knew your fear was real." Iblis gritted his teeth but could do nothing as the guards still held him.

As Aalon walked to me he began to tear up.

"Thank you," he whispered. "Thank you so much."

"Tell them what you want," I said. I wiped my own tears as slowly he approached the council podium.

"I want to thank Erin, Athyna, Jericho and many others who practiced what the humans call faith on my behalf. If it pleases the court, I'd like to request that my assignment Sean Logan be given entry to heaven and also the human soul of

Lorna the servant girl."

"Absolutely not!" Iblis tried to break free from his hold but couldn't. "Sean, fine! But Lorna belongs to me and has nothing to do with this." He again struggled and screamed. He almost broke loose. The angels tightened their hold until Iblis realized the struggle was in vain.

"Lorna is being tortured right now because of me and it is now on record that I should not have been there."

"I will not give you Lorna." Iblis echoed.

"Aalon, she is not in the book," the head Angel said. "Iblis would have to give her freely or-"

Iblis laughed. "She will pay for this. Oh she will pay. I'll do my best to see that you hear her screams in heaven."

"She can have my place here," he responded, surprising the entire courtroom - even me.

"Aalon, if you give up your stay in heaven, you can never return" the head council member said. "Please reconsider, you hardly know her."

Aalon walked to Athyna and with the saddest look and hugged her as if to say goodbye, "I will not live my life knowing Lorna receives torture and punishment for helping me," he said. "I will leave this heaven so she can enter."

"NO!" Iblis yelled. "Then Aalon belongs to me!"

"Silence!" the head angel yelled. "Aalon are you sure?"

Aalon hung his head. "I'm a guardian," he answered. "I was created for this."

"As you wish. Aalon from this day forward you will no longer be allowed to enter these gates. You've given up your place here in exchange for Lorna's entry."

Aalon turned to face Athyna as Sean and Lorna appeared. Their wounds healed almost instantaneously before us. Two angels came to their side. Athyna ran over to Aalon and hugged him tightly.

"Thank you," he whispered to me. While he began to disappear, Athyna screamed as loud as she could and fell to her knees and then Aalon was no longer among us.

CHAPTER 46

Audrey walked closer to Erin to make sure she wasn't mistaken. It looked like Erin's hand moved. She watched it again and waited. She saw her eyes flutter. And again her hand moved. She hit the button to page the nurse.

"It could mean she's coming out of it," the nurse said over the intercom. " I'll be in with the doctor."

EVEN *Angels* NEED MIRACLES

CHAPTER 47

Tears filled the room as angels recognized the finality of seeing their brother Aalon. There was joy for Sean and Lorna, but they could not get over the loss. Iblis and his team of hooded assistants prepared to leave. Surprisingly Iblis handled his defeat better than expected. He walked to me and extended his hand. "You performed brilliantly and I underestimated your abilities."

After refusing to shake his hand -- again, he returned it back to his side.

"Strange, a minute ago you threatened to kill me," I said.

"Just theatrics. Remember, I've yet to kill anyone. Even the person I tried to kill came back to life."

"But we'll be on our way. Kevin is in good hands."

I didn't believe my ears. It almost sounded like he said Kevin.

I stood there more confused than ever. He could tell I wasn't getting it.

"Damien, send the other here." Damien, the tall hooded figure sent the shorter figure over. "Remove your hood."

The hands came up to slowly grab the sides of his hood. When he lowered it completely Kevin stood before me. He looked saddened and sort of dazed.

I screamed at the top of my lungs as I charged toward him and held him in a tight hug.

"What did you do?" I yelled. "What did you do?"

He didn't answer. He stared as if he were ashamed. "I'm sorry," he finally said. "I love you."

"Athyna!" I screamed. Athyna removed herself from her hug with Jericho, Sean and Lorna. She quickly walked over. Jericho was not too far behind.

"There is nothing you can do," Iblis said. He held up Kevin's signature in blood, walked over to the head angel and slammed the contract on the lectern in a ferocious fashion. "He freely made the deal with me. Now I admit, he didn't know what he was signing, but oh well, he's a lawyer. He should have read the fine print."

I grabbed Kevin's arm. "No!" I shouted. I turned to the council. "This isn't right. Do something! Do something!"

"There's nothing they can do. His soul belongs to me!"

"I don't know why he would have done it, but if it's true there is nothing we can do," Athyna said.

"That's wrong! I did everything to help your friend and mine has to suffer!"

"Erin, it's not like that. If there was something," I pushed Athyna aside.

I walked to Kevin and slapped him. "I'm sorry," he said. His tears were trailing heavily. I hugged him again.

"I love you Kevin! I love you!"

"Where was his guardian?" I fell to my knees then to my face and cried.

"You can't win them all," Iblis said in a laughter as he walked past me. "Bring him."

"Wait!" I held Kevin in my stare. "You can have me." I wiped the tears from my face.

Athyna stooped down in front of me, "No! What are you doing," she yelled.

Iblis paused in mid stride and turned around. I walked toward Iblis in anger.

"You heard me," I said. "You can have me."

"No!" Kevin yelled. "Erin don't!"

Iblis closed his eyes to savor the moment. Though I knew better, it almost looked like he was praying.

"You heard her, she has willingly given her soul to me," he yelled. He shoved Kevin into Jericho. "Deal!" He grabbed me by my collar. "You will suffer unimaginable pain." Lorna, Sean and every angel in the room showed complete desperation on their faces, but they were powerless I was scared out of my mind and tried to find comfort in knowing Kevin would be fine.

"Come," he said. His servant quickly grabbed me and walked me briskly behind Iblis.

"Can't any of you do anything?" Kevin yelled. "Anyone!"

"You're no longer needed!" Iblis said calmly. He waived his hand and Kevin disappeared before us.

A dark opening formed in the floor in front of me. I could feel the heat. I could hear the screams and smell the stench.

With tears, I turned around to see everyone for the last time. Iblis stepped aside and stood close behind me. "Enjoy your new home," he said as he gave a huge shove, but amazingly as forceful as the shove was I didn't budge. "I said get in there!" He pushed again with all his might yet surprisingly I stood firmly.

"Excuse me," said the elder angel as he pointed to the opened pages of a large glowing book on his lectern. "But her soul already belongs to someone else." The books glow became brighter to the point where it was almost blinding. "Apparently, her soul has been a part of this book since many years ago."

"No!!" Iblis yelled at the top of his lungs. "Then Kevin returns back to me!"

The pages of the book turned by themselves, "Actually his name is also here." It wasn't totally obvious, but the elder angel seemed to smile at the news. He held Iblis' contract and compared it with the book writing. "It seems it was written only a few moments before your own contract. Immediately, his contract burned to nothing. Jericho slowly walked closer and closer to Iblis. I felt a strong release of tension and was able to free myself from Iblis' grasp. I walked over to Athyna and the rest of the group.

"So I leave with nothing!" Iblis yelled. Jericho approached closer still, "What about my freedom? Since we're in the mood to free those trapped in hell. Can't we reason this out?"

"Lucifer! Demons can never be reasoned with," Jericho yelled. At this point, he was standing in Iblis' face. "Only one way to come to terms with a demon."

"And what is that? I demand to know."

"Demons must be cast out!" Jericho grabbed Iblis by his clothing and his hooded assistant and hurled them into the dark hole and it immediately closed.

We all shouted in joy. Athyna walked to me. "You showed amazing courage and love. I am so thankful for you. She hugged me tight. "You have taught me and every angel here, what it means to have faith and that even though we can't see the outcome, we can have victory. May your spirit always remember and may you always know that even though I'm not your guardian, I will always be in your court - forever ."

CHAPTER 48

Iblis walked into his quarters enraged. He wanted revenge. He turned to the hooded fallen angel behind him.

He grabbed him by the throat. "Bring me Aalon!" he growled. "He is of the utmost priority."

"Yes master," he said and disappeared.

"You were wonderful, I heard." My grandma said.

"Thanks. If you were there, you wouldn't think I did that great."

"Baby, I think everything you do is great."

"I know you are happy, grandma. But-"

"But what?"

"I guess I just need to hear that you are."

"Baby, I am happy; and I'm even more happy that you are well," she said.

"I miss you so much."

"I know. And I miss you. But don't worry about me. You just continue to live your life as you are doing," she said. "That's what makes me happy. To see you doing the things you enjoy and not worrying about me. Promise me you will continue to do that."

"I promise," I said.

The tears began to fall between both us as we embraced.

"I thought there are no more tears in heaven," I said.

"These are the good kind," she said.

We held our hug for a quiet moment and shortly, she vanished away.

"Erin," Athyna's voice said from behind.

"Let me guess. It's time, right?"

"Unless you planned on staying here," Jericho said jokingly.

"Is it even possible?" I asked.

"Are you still asking about possibilities?" Athyna said.

I guess with all that's taken place, asking what is possible and what's not does register as silly.

"I have so many questions." I turned to Athyna. "What will happen to Aalon?"

"I don't know," Athyna said. "I have to trust he knew the meaning of his sacrifice."

"Is he in-"

"I don't know. All I know is he is no longer here." She interrupted. "I pray he's not there."

"But he traded places with her," I asked.

"No! He only gave up being here," she replied. She looked at Jericho for confirmation. He nodded but didn't' do it convincingly. "He could be anywhere."

I closed my eyes and hoped for the best for him. "I won't remember any of this will I?"

Athyna turned to look at Jericho for the answer.

"I can't say. We've never done this before. I can say though there have been times before when angels have intervened in humans lives and some were able to remember and some were not. I think you will retain what's important to retain."

"How will this work?" I asked.

"It will be quick and unexpected."

"Thank you." Athyna said. She held my hand.

"Thank you for helping." Jericho said.

"Thank you for believing," said Athyna.

I sat down and took in the room.

"Am I supposed to just close my eyes and I'll be whisked away? Do I go to sleep and wake up home? How will it happen?"

CHAPTER 49

"Where is he?" Iblis looked at the fallen angel as he entered his chambers. Iblis sat at his thrown. His face showed no less intensity than when he first came from the trial. The fallen angel's face showed absolute fear to the point of trembling.

"Master he is not here."

"WHAT!" Iblis stood up and turned his thrown on its side.

"We have looked everywhere. Master, I've put out searchers across your kingdom. No sign of him at all.

"NOOOO!" Iblis stormed to the fallen angel and beat him until nothing was there.

"Are you sure!" said the muffled voice.

"Yes! Yes! She squeezed my hand. I felt it." Audrey said.

"I could barely open my eyes. The light in the room was so bright it stung.

My throat and mouth felt so dry. The breathing tube in my nose was very uncomfortable.

"Erin, can you hear me?"

I tried again to open my eyes. This time I kept them open no matter how bad they hurt. They started to water and that's when Audrey's face came into focus.

"Thank you Jesus! She opened her eyes."

CHAPTER 50

Forty five days later ...

"Thank you Erin. Thank you so much."

"It's my pleasure to take your case," I said to Ms. Emily. "If that developer wants to seize and demolish your house to put up that shopping center, they are going to have to go through me."

Audrey walked in the door carrying a phone memo and waiving it frantically like it was an emergency. On it she wrote someone's phone number. She set it on my desk.

"What's this?" I whispered.

"It's Kevin's new cell number. He said to call him back. It's urgent."

Since my accident Kevin and I have become closer – you could say we are dating. He resigned from his firm a few days after regaining consciousness. It hurt him to leave when he was so close to becoming partner, but he didn't appreciate the firm's willingness to risk his being disbarred or threatened with violece to represent Antonio Walker, who was found guilty and received a life sentence. He's been interviewing with several other top notch firms in the area. I still find it amazing how he fell into a diabetic coma around the same time and regained consciousness just several hours before I awoke. I took the note and stuck it to my monitor to remind me to call him back.

"Should I call you back," Ms. Emily questioned. She could overhear me talking to Audrey about Kevin. She was in the middle of talking about the history of her house and all the children she raised over the years.

"I'm sorry," I said sincerely. "I was talking to someone in my office, if you don't mind, do I have to get off the phone and make another phone call."

Ms. Emily thanked me again and said good bye. I almost forgot that she was a talker.

"What does Kevin want?"

"How should I know?" Audrey asked. "I'm just the messenger. But you should call him back. He sounded like he was excited. Maybe he landed with that firm in D.C." She tapped her watch to remind me she was leaving for class.

"I stood up to go to the fax machine and felt woozy. I had to brace myself against the credenza.

"Erin!" Audrey shouted as she ran over to support me. "Are you okay?"

Ever since the accident, I've been experiencing a few dizzy spells. The doctor said it was normal, but I should take it slow with work, until the spells went completely away.

"Why are you rushing?" Audrey said. "Remember you need to pace yourself. No point in having you back if you work yourself into another coma."

I still hadn't gotten use to me missing nearly two weeks of my life. The whole time came and went without my remembering as much as a dream. Very strange.

I sat down.

"You want me to skip my class?" She asked obviously concerned about me.

"No, I'll be all right."

She looked at me.

"Seriously?" I asked. "I'll be fine."

She hesitated to leave.

"If I cancel my meetings, would that make you feel better."

"Nope, but I'd feel better if I cancelled them," she said. "I'll do it before I leave."

I can't say I was that upset. I needed a light day. After my accident - I was out a good month - it's been nonstop appointments and deadlines since day one. My car was totaled from the water damage. I just received my insurance check and thought about getting me something nicer.

"Goodbye sis," Audrey yelled from the lobby before leaving. I heard the little bell chime ring as she opened the door. "You have a visitor!" She yelled.

Who now? I thought. I know I didn't have any appointments for this hour. I stood up and walked from my office to the front lobby. It was a dressed-down Kevin. He looked just as good without his power suit.

"I thought you wanted me to call," I said.

"Actually," he said. "I needed to see you in person." He gave me a kiss.

He led me to the lobby sofa and sat down.

"I've been offered a position at the Piper firm."

"That's great Kevin," I said. I gave him a hug.

"That's what I thought," he said. "But I declined."

"You what? That is a nice firm. You would do well there."

"I know," he said. "But it's not me any longer. I just feel like I have a higher calling and well."

"Well what?" I asked.

"I thought I could join your practice."

I laughed. "Are you joking?" I asked.

"Actually, I'm serious."

"Wow," I whispered. I stood up but felt woozy and almost fell to the floor, before Kevin caught me.

"You okay?" he asked. "I know it's shocking news, but I didn't think you'd faint."

"It's not this," I said. "It's these recurring dizzy spells. I thought I was getting better, but maybe I am rushing it."

He walked to the mini fridge to bring me some water.

"You know, we've never really spoken about our experience," he started and cut himself short. "I'm glad you came out of it okay."

"Me too." I said.

"Any memories," I asked.

"Nope."

"Me neither," I said. "Strange."

"So, can an out-of-work lawyer get a job?" Kevin asked.

I needed the help, I thought. Kevin was a great lawyer. Probably better than me truth be told. "Truth is, I don't need any lawyers working for me," I said. "But I could use a partner. Welcome aboard."

Two Weeks Later ...

Audrey, Kevin and I sat down. I was surprised at how busy the restaurant was for a Tuesday evening. We waited for almost an hour to be seated. In celebration of our win for Ms. Emily and our first case together, we came to Porters, a popular Bistro in a trendy neighborhood in the southern part of the city. Ms. Emily was equally excited, but couldn't join us. Not only did we succeed in defending her home, but the city ruled that the developer find a new location for their shopping center and that her home was located in a historic district. This meant, her home was protected from other future developers. As we looked over our menu, I thought of how great it was to have Kevin as part of the team not just for this win but for the firm. As a partner, he helped me catch up on some overdue bills and get the firm back on solid financial footing. The goal was to build the firm over the next few years to add a few more attorneys and interns looking to build an honest reputation in their practice.

We ordered our meals and gave the menu back.

"Oh, may we have a bottle of Sebastiani," I asked the server.

"Of course. I'll be back with your wine madam."

"We are celebrating, right?" I asked Audrey and Kevin.

"Hey, that's how I see it," Kevin responded.

As the night progressed, we ate our dinner and talked about our first victory together. A few short stories and lots of laughter filled the hours leaving us among the last few tables left before closing. As we were eating dessert, I could tell we all were starting to get tired. "I've got to go to the ladies room," Audrey said. "Excuse me."

I checked her out to make sure her walking didn't take on an inebriated stumble or lean. As she walked away Kevin whispered to me.

"Erin I want to share this with you," he whispered while leaving "when I was in the coma, I did have a dream about you." He gently grabbed my hand.

"Oh really?" I laughed.

"No really. It was weird." He said. You were like an angel or something."

I laughed more.

"Sir, ma'am, can I get you anything else?"

"I think you have the wrong table," Kevin said apologetically.

"Oh your server is gone for the evening and I'm helping to close her station," she said.

"Well, you can bring us the check." I said. "Should I leave the tip with you? Uh…"

"Athyna," she said.

"Should I leave the tip with you Athyna?"

"Aren't you the two who helped that kind woman today in court?" She asked.

"Ms. Emily?" Kevin asked.

"Yes, I know her." Athyna said. "She's a kind woman. Tell you what. Your dinner is on the house tonight."

I looked at her strangely. "You know we're lawyers right? You can't just joke like that – at least around me."

"No joking. The meal is free. Enjoy."

"Why are you giving us a free meal?" Kevin interrupted. "Cause you know her?"

"Yes, but who knows, I may need lawyers like you two in the future."

"Thanks," I said. "Although something about her comment made me feel like she was being extra honest in that statement.

"No, the thanks should go to you."

Athyna walked back in the kitchen. Something familiar struck me about her, but I couldn't put my finger on it. I eventually dismissed the feeling.

"This turned out to be a good day." I said.

"Yeah, I think you and I may have plenty of days like this ahead of us," Kevin said while leaning back in his chair a bit, his smile still as affectionate as ever.

"Here! Here!" I said

We toasted briefly interrupting the silence of an empty restaurant with the high pitch cling of our glasses.

"Did I miss something?" Audrey said as she sat back down. She reached for her glass a bit too late for joining the toast.

"Nothing," Kevin said after his sip. He raised his glass again to cling with Audrey.

"We just received a free meal for doing our job." Kevin said.

THE JOURNEY CONTINUES

For four days I've sat here watching. Just watching and thinking. People are never aware that they are constantly being watched – by each other and by "us." Though, now that I think about it, I guess I'm no longer included in us anymore. Literally and spiritually, I'm not sure how I made it to this point. One moment, I'm home embracing my family and the next place I find myself is here – a flat rooftop on a deserted building. Again, I peered over the side looking at the void cityscape. If memory serves me correctly, it's about March, a month that still holds a few cold and freezing nights. Tonight was no exception. Not even the rats were moving about. The empty streets made for an eerie, yet peaceful 3:00 a.m.

Unlike it is now, throughout the day, there's chaos - chaos around people and within. I know first-hand how people go about from day to day, fighting hard to keep people from knowing who they really are, or what they're really dealing with.

As expected, walking down the street is the same young teenager. Every night since I've been here, he's walked this route undisturbed. This time, however, he seems more nervous as he methodically keeps checking over his shoulder as if to make sure no one is following.

A pair of headlights shine as they turn onto the same street. The driver turns the lights off and slowly rolls up to Justin "Hey punk! How much you got on you?" The driver angled the car on the sidewalk blocking Justin's path and stepped out of the car to approach the teenager.

"I don't have anything man," Justin said, his hands still in his pockets.

Not buying the teen's answer, the man, knowing no one was around at this time of night, reached behind to the small of his back and pulled out a gun.

"We'll see about that." He pushed Justin against the side of the building and reached into Justin's pocket and pulled out some folded up bills.

"Hey man, I need that money." Justin said.

"Shut up!" he slapped him across his head knocking off his baseball cap.

In the few days I've been here, I've watched a few misdeeds take place, including watching someone break into a car and steal a few items, I witnessed someone drop some money and another pick it up, even saw someone get out of a cab and take off without paying. This however, was different. I wasn't created to simply watch this. Not knowing whether I'd fly, fall or safely land, I placed my hands on the ledge of the eight story building and leaped to help.

ABOUT A.C. MOORE

New to the world of fiction, acclaimed writer and communications professional A.C. Moore brings unique, exciting and tasteful stories to reading lovers.

A.C. likes to describe his writing style as fresh storytelling with a keen ability of building intimacy and interaction between his readers and his characters. As a Christian, husband, and father, he prides himself on including plenty of authenticity and description, yet keeping his stories free from obscenities and unnecessary detail.

Growing up and now working in the Baltimore / Washington, DC Metropolitan area, A.C. discovered his dream of becoming an author early in his childhood. A fan of creative writing courses and assignments, he flourished in school and began to apply his talent in the workforce.

Countless published writings and awards followed him throughout his education and career. He graduated from Morgan State University in Baltimore and earned his Bachelor's degree in Mass Communications. He has since worked in several writing, public relations and marketing environments where he has written and served as spokes persons for several businesses and nonprofits.

Currently, A.C. is pursuing a Master's degree in Communications from Johns Hopkins University. He also has a part time marketing and communications business.

For more on A.C. Moore or to tell him about you, visit MooreNovels.com